She Walks in Beauty

More Belt Revivals

Poor White by Sherwood Anderson

Main-Travelled Roads by Hamlin Garland

The History of the Standard Oil Company by Ida Tarbell

The Damnation of Theron Ware by Harold Frederic

Stories from Ohio by William Dean Howells

The Artificial Man and Other Stories by Clare Winger Harris

The Marrow of Tradition by Charles W. Chesnutt

The Shame of the Cities by Lincoln Steffens

One of Ours by Willa Cather

The Girls by Edna Ferber

The Fastest Bicycle Rider in the World by Marshall W. "Major" Taylor

She Walks in Beauty

Dawn Powell

Introduction copyright © 2025, Ilana Masad
All rights reserved. This introduction or any portion thereof may not be reproduced or used in any manner whatsoever without the express written permission of the publisher except for the use of brief quotations in a book review.

First Belt Publishing Edition 2025
ISBN: 9781953368959

Belt Publishing
6101 Penn Avenue, Suite 201, Pittsburgh, PA 15206
www.beltpublishing.com

Cover by David Wilson

Contents

Introduction, by Ilana Masad ix

Chapter One 3
Chapter Two 33
Chapter Three 68
Chapter Four 94
Chapter Five 109
Chapter Six 127
Chapter Seven 137
Chapter Eight 147
Chapter Nine 161
Chapter Ten 177
Chapter Eleven 200

About the Author 205

Introduction

There is much to be said in praise of Dawn Powell, and many—although not enough—have said it better than I ever could. In her own day she was admired by Ernest Hemingway, Edmund Wilson, and editor Maxwell Perkins and kept company with them and other literary luminaries like E. E. Cummings and John Dos Passos in Greenwich Village. Decades after her death, Gore Vidal called her "that unthinkable monster, a witty woman who felt no obligation to make a single, much less final, down payment on Love or The Family." More recently, Rachel Syme has called her the epitome of the writer's writer, saying she "wrote with the kind of highly attuned, neurotic, slashing wit that others in the business love—she struck out at her craft, her contemporaries, and her own ambitions, and she aimed for the heart." Fran Lebowitz told an interviewer that there was no writer she could "recommend more heartily" and further opined that in reading Powell's diaries, you'll "see what it really means to be a writer." Academy Award winner Anjelica Huston has long wanted to adapt Powell's books and is devoted enough

Introduction

that she's said if anyone dares do it without her, "they'll have hell to pay." *Gilmore Girls* creator Amy Sherman-Palladino worked praise of the author into an episode.

Despite these varied endorsements of her work, what Vidal wrote in 1987 still rings true: "Dawn Powell was always just on the verge of ceasing to be a cult and becoming a major religion." More of her books are in print now than they were when Vidal reintroduced her to the reading public, and critic Tim Page has worked hard to bring her posthumous notoriety, publishing her biography and an edited collection of her diaries as well as editing the two Library of America volumes encompassing nine of her novels. Yet I'd wager that far more people have heard of Powell's contemporary wit Dorothy Parker. Even if you *have* heard of Dawn Powell, you're probably familiar with her deliciously biting and wickedly funny New York novels, which were reissued in the late 1990s with wonderfully eye-catching art deco–ish covers by Steerforth Press.

The book you hold in your hands is quite different.

She Walks in Beauty is the first of Dawn Powell's Ohio cycle, a set of novels that all take place in her Midwestern state of origin. Born in Mount Gilead in 1896, Powell met with hardship early in the form of her mother's death in 1903, rumored to have been caused by a botched abortion. She and her siblings were shuffled around to various relatives while their father, a salesman, traveled for work until he remarried and settled the family near Cleveland. As a young teenager, after her abusive stepmother burned some of her notebooks, Powell left home to live with an aunt in Shelby, where she was able to go to high school and nurture her precocious literary ambitions. After graduating, she attended Lake Erie College, where she wrote, acted, edited the school newspaper, and generally seemed to enjoy herself outside of the classroom much more than in it. Once she'd earned her degree, she lived in Connecticut briefly before finally moving to the city that would become one of the great loves of her life: New York.

By the time she wrote *She Walks in Beauty* in 1925, Powell was married to Joseph Gousha, a fellow writer, and had given birth to her only child, Jojo, whom her biographer Tim Page believes was autistic rather than intellectually disabled and schizophrenic, the diagnoses he received during his lifetime. Her relationships with both husband and son were complicated. She and Gousha would fight and come back together, and each had affairs throughout their marriage; they lived fairly separate lives. As for Jojo, he was an intelligent and sensitive child but also prone to throwing inconsolable tantrums and, when he grew older, to fits of violence. Powell loved him, but she and Gousha also "had absolutely no idea what to do with" him, according to Page. Jojo spent many of his early years with a dedicated nurse and later lived mostly in schools and institutions, with occasional periods back home with his parents.

Powell worked throughout her adult life, writing book reviews, short stories, plays, and novels, but despite the literary circles she moved in—and sent up in her New York cycle—she never quite made it in the way she wanted to. By the time she died of intestinal cancer in 1965, almost all her books were already out of print. She outlived her husband, and in her hastily made will, she donated her body to science and designated a friend, Jacqueline Miller Rice, as her executor. When science, in the form of the Cornell Medical Center, was finished with Powell's remains, Rice made no moves to return them to Powell's family but rather allowed them to be buried on Hart Island, New York City's public cemetery.

She Walks in Beauty was published in 1928 and was, technically, Powell's second novel, but she called it and promoted it as her first, having disavowed her actual debut, *Wither*, nearly as soon as it was published. It takes place in the fictional town of Birchfield during the

Introduction

couple years leading up to the Great War and follows two sisters, Linda and Dorrie, who live with their grandmother, called Aunt Jule by all, in the boardinghouse she runs across from the railroad station.

The book opens with Linda walking down Maple Avenue "with her smooth blonde head held stiffly erect, her resentful blue eyes fixed straight ahead." Beautiful and bitter, Linda is disgusted with her circumstances, hates living in a filthy boardinghouse with people she considers trashy, and aspires to nothing more than to be considered respectable by Birchfield's small and snobby elite. Dorrie, on the other hand, is an enthusiastic resident of Aunt Jule's, always romanticizing the other lodgers and eager to meet whatever travelers come to stay.

Reviews of the novel were mixed. Many praised the writing itself but criticized nearly everything else. "It has neither point, integration, nor form," read a review in *The Nation*; another, in the *New York Herald Tribune*, said that "the serious weakness of this book lies in its having no point." The *Saturday Review* decided, bizarrely, that "books with as much merit as 'She Walks in Beauty' come in for harsher criticism than their inferior contemporaries, because they say so briskly and explicitly what they want to say that one cannot help wishing they wanted to say something more important."

More amusingly, *The Independent*'s critic wrote, "The cover jacket compares her, not unfavorably, with Sinclair Lewis, Sherwood Anderson, and Edgar Lee Masters. Nevertheless, her book is good." *The New Republic* appreciated that "Miss Powell wisely refrains from pointing any moral." *The New York Times*, in two different reviews, opined that "Miss Powell has the gift of the incisive stroke; she doesn't need much space to build a human being out of printer's ink" and that "for all its occasional simperings of style, it captures the mood or moods of youth growing up in a small town."

It's true that *She Walks in Beauty* is somewhat less polished than Powell's later novels, but therein lies its charm; it's exploratory, a great and sincere attempt that throws many characters at the proverbial wall and tries to make them all stick fast. At the same time, it's confident in its sense of place, which is fixed and specific and quite possibly drawn from real life, as Powell's own aunt ran a boardinghouse where she lived for some time. The author's voice is still maturing and developing in this book, but what became its essence—a dry wit and a willingness to poke fun at human weaknesses—is already present.

She Walks in Beauty's plot is subtle but existent, and it concerns the shifting positions of Linda and Dorrie, both within the town and their imagined—even manifested—futures. Along the way, Powell treats us to a steady stream of anecdotes, each revealing something about the sisters through their reactions to and interactions with the characters peopling the boardinghouse.

Over the course of the novel, readers meet a few dozen characters—Aunt Jule's boarders, Birchfield's haughtiest and plainest residents, and a couple out-of-town family members—who range in class, occupation, age, and attitude. Powell has been said to be cynical, but there is warmth and tenderness in her observations of the ridiculous. She was especially enamored, I think, with how often people lie to themselves and how transparent we all are about it. Whether it's boardinghouse lodger Ella Morris repeatedly implying that the respectable men who visit are secretly in love with her, Mrs. Stall's belief that her daughter Gertrude is a genius at the piano, or Aunt Jule's refusal to admit that Esther Mason is constantly cheating on her husband, Powell delights in making fun of them without the slightest moralizing tone. It's human, she seems to be saying, to be a little deluded; how are we to face life's hardships if we don't let ourselves live in our fantasies some of the time?

Introduction

Birchfield itself plays a great role in the book, and just as she does with her characters, Powell presents it with both love and mockery. Although it isn't real, its reference points are particular to Ohio and the Midwest. Near Aunt Jule's runs the B&O, or the Baltimore and Ohio Railroad, the oldest of its kind in the United States. Courtenay Stall, whom Linda is in love with, is forever taking girls from Lima or Cleveland around in his car. And to the extremely Midwestern Birchfield, Powell writes, "New York was as meaningless and remote as a billion dollars—Akron or even Mansfield meaning far more to them as a symbol of culture—still, New York was East, and, as East, Birchfield bowed to it." Even Dorrie, the dreamer, stays close to home in her fantasies. "How wonderful," she thinks, "if she could join a company some day when it came to her grandmother's, and go to strange exotic places like South Bend, Dayton, or even Louisville."

The town can be as small or as large as its people, and it represents a great deal of different things to its varied residents. To Marie Farley, originally from New York City, it's a backwater whose bakers have tragically never heard of chocolate éclairs; to Esther Mason, who's spent her life on a farm, "Birchfield was Paris," a real city; to Mr. and Mrs. Winslow, out-of-work actors who've ended up staying rather longer than planned at Aunt Jule's, Birchfield is a lovely place to settle down, except that they don't seem to actually want to. It's all relative, Powell knows; indeed, in her later novels she impeccably captured how New York City can be as provincial as any Midwestern town, just as here she captures how such a town can be as captivating, fascinating, and full of drama as that famous city.

Ilana Masad
February 2025

Works Cited

Chamberlain, John R. "Six Months in the Field of Fiction." *The New York Times*, June 24, 1928.

"Fiction Shorts." *The Nation* 126, no. 3283 (June 6, 1928).

"Fran Lebowitz on New York Writers." Five Books. https://fivebooks.com/best-books/fran-lebowitz-on-new-york-writers/.

Hazel, Mycah. "Her Writing Was Admired by Hemingway. Then Her Books—and Body—Disappeared." NPR, October 30, 2023. https://www.npr.org/2023/10/30/1208533790/dawn-powell-writer-new-york-radio-diaries-hart-island.

Latimer, Margery. "The Agony of Growing." *New York Herald Tribune*, April 15, 1928.

Library of America. "The Library of America Presents: Dawn Powell." October 14, 2007. https://web.archive.org/web/20071014045757/http://loa.org/dawnpowell/.

"The New Books." *The Saturday Review of Literature* 4, no. 42 (May 12, 1928). http://archive.org/details/sim_saturday-review_1928-05-12_4_42_0.

"New Books in Brief Review." *The Independent*, April 28, 1928. http://archive.org/details/sim_independent_1928-04-28_120_4065.

Page, Tim. *Dawn Powell: A Biography*. Henry Holt, 1998. http://archive.org/details/dawnpowellbiogr00page.

———. "Who Was Dawn Powell?" The Diaries of Dawn Powell, May 12, 2012. https://www.dawnpowelldiaries.com/who-was-dawn-powell/.

Rayfield, Jillian. "Dawn Powell's Writing Has Been Rediscovered. What About Her Grave?" *The New York Times*, September 29, 2023. https://www.nytimes.com/2023/09/29/arts/dawn-powell-hart-island.html.

"'She Walks in Beauty' and Other Works of Fiction." *The New York Times*, March 25, 1928.

Syme, Rachel. "Dawn Powell's Masterful Gossip: Why Won't It Sell?" *The New Yorker*, July 23, 2012. https://www.newyorker.com/books/page-turner/dawn-powells-masterful-gossip-why-wont-it-sell.

Introduction

Tonguette, Peter. "The Triumphs and Tragedies of Dawn Powell, Central Ohio's Forgotten Literary Genius." *Columbus Monthly*, November 16, 2021. https://www.columbusmonthly.com/story/lifestyle/features/2021/11/16/ohio-novelist-dawn-powell-a-time-to-be-born-my-home-is-far-away-author/6387725001/.

Vidal, Gore. "Dawn Powell, the American Writer." *The New York Review of Books* 34, no. 17 (November 5, 1987). https://www.nybooks.com/articles/1987/11/05/dawn-powell-the-american-writer/.

———. "Queen of the Golden Age." *The New York Review of Books* 43, no. 5 (March 21, 1996). https://www.nybooks.com/articles/1996/03/21/queen-of-the-golden-age/.

Walter, Laura Maylene, and Jennifer Swartz-Levine. "Rediscovering Dawn Powell." *Page Count* podcast, June 4, 2004. https://ohiocenterforthebook.org/podcast/rediscovering-dawn-powell/.

Walton, Edith H. Review of *She Walks in Beauty*, by Dawn Powell. The New Republic 54, no 700 (May 2, 1928). *Internet Archive*, http://archive.org/details/sim_new-republic_1928-05-02_54_700.

She Walks in Beauty

Chapter One

Linda always walked down Maple Avenue with her smooth blonde head held stiffly erect, her resentful blue eyes fixed straight ahead. When she reached the corner poolroom, a deep red mounted her face, beginning at the back of her neck and tingling slowly around and up. She was conscious of eyes—men's eyes, leering and red-rimmed like Tim Cruger's, and of smokeveiled whispers.

Linda's heels clacked on the pavement, each step an agony, reverberating far down the street from one end of Birchfield to the other, tapping out—

"Linda Shirley from Aunt Jule's! Linda Shirley from Aunt Jule's! Trash!"

Then as she left the paved respectability of Maple Avenue and approached the alley leading to the tumbled South End, Linda's pace slowed. Her head drooped. Bitterness came into her eyes.

Beyond the tracks there sprawled the railroad buildings, the roundhouse, the freight barn. Back a little from the road stood Lew Mason's livery stable, with huge white letters painted on its roof:

VISIT MAY'S BIG STORE.

Almost hidden by the birches on the other side of the road was Red Turner's Quick Lunch Shack. You could see his big sign nailed to a tree in front:

Dinner 35¢
STEP IN

Sometimes traveling salesmen, stranded actresses, even tramps, would stop at Red's for information about lodgings. Red, his white apron

3

modestly stuffed into his pants' pocket, would take the wanderer by the elbow to the door of the shack and point down the road.

"See that big house just above the birches? That's Jule's place. Aunt Jule, folks call her. Just you run over there and maybe she'll find a bed for you. Cheap, too. The house may be full but she'll have a place for one more. Plenty of cots and folding beds in her garret. Sure. No trouble at all."

Jule's was a huge old square house painted a dull charcoal by time and the B & O. A narrow porch was thrust out in front like a sullen underlip. Over it, a great oak leaned a protective elbow. Elderberry bushes obscured the side of the house, yet a row of garbage and ash cans always managed to peep triumphantly out of the foliage. The grass was always high and uneven in the front yard. Tim Cruger was supposed to mow it every Saturday, but invariably he smelt a drink in the midst of the job and left to follow his unerring nose. Up by the front steps a scraggy vine attempted to reach the porch railing but grew discouraged a few inches above the trellising and dropped a barren and exhausted shoot back to earth.

The windows were discreetly curtained with the white lace of the period. In one—it was Mr. Wickley's attic room—hung a shriveled Christmas wreath. Mr. Wickley, never having noticed it when Aunt Jule put it up, naturally never thought of taking it down. In the window of the parlor bedroom, Aunt Jule's room except when the house was full of boarders, gallantly clung the campaign photograph of Theodore Roosevelt as it had clung for the last six years. You could tell Linda's room because the shade was always lowered.

Linda recognized from afar Ella and Mr. Tompkins in the rockers out under the oak tree. Ella was an invalid and was the only person who attracted callers to Jule's from Birchfield's "nice people," and these came out of benign charity. After all, Ella was a niece of old Senator Morris . . .

"She hopes I'll see her entertaining the president of the bank," Linda thought in disgust. "I'll not give her the satisfaction of looking . . . just go in the back way."

She hurried behind Red Turner's shack, ignoring his "Hullo, Linda, how's Aunt Jule?" and turned into the leafy lane running to Jule's backyard. In the shadow of the young pear trees she caught a glimpse of a slight figure in green gingham—Dorrie, of course. And Dorrie at that moment was lifting her lips, her eyes closed, to the smelly boy called Steve from the livery stable.

Linda clenched her teeth. What if Mr. Tompkins should chance to see that? Oh, wasn't it enough that she should be cursed by the shadow of that black ghastly house without her own sister helping to drag her further down?

"Bye, Dorrie," called Steve wistfully.

Dorrie waved her handkerchief and skipped toward the house without seeing Linda. She didn't like Steve, of course, but he was going to run away to sea, and when he talked about it, Dorrie had only to close her eyes and imagine him a gallant naval officer in a thrilling blue cape, swinging down lazy tropical streets . . . bazaars . . . date palms . . . clatter of a royal coach . . . Andalusian skies . . .

At the moment of the kiss, Dorrie was fancying herself the belle of Madrid, coquetting with this jaunty American naval officer. Indeed, though Linda missed the gesture, as Dorrie left Steve, she was delicately fluttering a perfumed, black lace fan . . .

"I saw you kiss that filthy boy," Linda hissed tensely, coming upon her young sister at the kitchen steps. "Have you no pride, Dorrie Shirley? Isn't there a spark of decency in the whole family? Bad enough to live in a house of riffraff—"

"Sh—sh—Grandma's in the kitchen."

"I don't care—without my own sister doing her best to make things worse!"

Linda whirled into the kitchen, refused her grandmother's cheerful salutation, and stalked upstairs to her room. Dorrie, somewhat scared, as she always was at Linda's cold rages, exchanged a startled glance with her grandmother as they heard the door bang overhead.

Dorrie's grandmother, known to Birchfield and all of her great family of lodgers past and present as Aunt Jule, was getting supper. She was a splendid woman, even now in her late sixties, a woman of magnificent physique, with a fine mellow face, handsome nose, gentle golden eyes, and a sensitive thoroughbred mouth. Aunt Jule had been a belle in her day—that much at least Birchfield admitted possible. But today she was a town character, a social outcast, as any woman must be who for a period of years keeps a cheap lodging house for the tangle of driftwood washed in by the railroad trains. Yet there was a noble dignity about her in her gray percale housedress, her black hair piled in sleek coils on the top of her head, and tiny curls lying on the back of her smooth olive neck.

She was preparing potatoes and silently handed Dorrie a knife.

"What were you doing to upset Linda?" she asked, her brown fingers deftly releasing a long shingle of potato skin.

"Not a thing," Dorrie said serenely.

Her grandmother looked relieved. She had seen the kiss from the kitchen window, but she really preferred Dorrie to fib about it since a confession would have necessitated a rebuke. Jule hated to have the peace ruffled by rebukes and discipline and quarrels. Linda's occasional furies she dreaded.

"Miss Bellows here yet?" Dorrie asked, sniffing the air to determine the menu for dinner. She caught a glimpse of a great black pot on the enormous gas range. "Noodles," she contentedly reflected. Noodles never failed to thrill Dorrie with a sublime ecstasy.

"Yes, she came today," Jule's voice always dropped to a pianissimo when she discussed the affairs of her house, although she never said anything but fantastically exaggerated praise of her roomers, things they would have been delighted if not astonished to hear.

"She's still teaching. She's in Shiloh on Mondays and Tuesdays, and goes to Crestline over Sundays, so she just wants a room for Thursdays and Fridays. I let her have the front bedroom upstairs."

"Has she any pupils in Birchfield?" Dorrie idly asked. She was thinking enviously of Miss Bellows, traveling about all week—Crestline, Shelby, Birchfield, and once a month to Mansfield! What a life of adventure! Miss Bellows, of course, was nearly thirty—too old to enjoy her opportunities. But if one were seventeen or eighteen—Dorrie wondered if she couldn't take music lessons someday and travel around teaching, like Miss Bellows—of course, after she had learned to cross her hands and play the "Album Leaf," you know, that hard piece on page thirty-nine.

"Not many pupils. She's moving her piano in. I said she might as well use ours, but she said she'd keep her own here. No place else, I guess."

Dorie thought this fair enough. The piano which Jule had offered was an old square grand, a stout little log holding up the corner where the leg had broken off. Several generations of mice had made their homes in the strings, so that only half a dozen notes sounded. Dorrie was wont to give spectacular recitals on this piano, unhampered by discords or her own ignorance of music.

Sometimes Aunt Jule asked a caller to sit down and play, and she adjusted her large person to the old carpet-seated rocker and rocked enjoyably to the rhythm of the practically noiseless composition. It was easy to understand Miss Bellows's refusal of the favor.

"I can let her room out the rest of the week," pursued Jule. "She won't mind. I may press out the sheets that are on the bed now. That man only slept there two nights."

Linda walked in. She had changed her blue office suit for a clean blue bungalow apron. Her eyes were dark with repressed anger, but the storm had passed.

Dorrie and Jule breathed a little more freely.

Linda lifted the lid of the noodle pot, banged it on again. She lifted the lid of the iron kettle.

"Grandma," she accused, "you haven't thrown away that stew yet. It's nothing but garbage! Look! Lima beans, corn, tomatoes, onions, potatoes, and string beans!—and green peppers and chopped beef and heaven knows what all. You put something new in every day. I declare it's not fit to eat!"

"It's good!" Dorrie defended her grandmother's cooking with honest enthusiasm. "Chile con carne, that's what it is."

"I doubt it," said Linda coldly.

She went to the huge yellow cupboard and got out dishes and silverware to put on the red-checkered tablecloth.

"As long as we've lived here you've always had a pot of something like that on the back of the stove that you threw all the leavings in and called chile con carne. I hate the stuff."

Dorrie and Jule silently peeled their potatoes. Jule got up and scooped a spoonful of grease from a jar at the back of the stove into the skillet.

"Anybody for the light-housekeeping rooms?" Linda asked, nodding toward the wing at the left consisting of the summer kitchen and a dark little bedroom.

Jule nodded. Dorrie, sensing calamity in her grandmother's pretended absorption in frying potatoes, looked up at her inquisitively.

"Who?" she whispered.

The old woman looked warningly in Linda's direction.

"Lew Mason and his new wife," she whispered back to Dorrie.

It was too loud a whisper.

"Lew Mason and his wife!" Linda repeated incredulously, the sugar bowl poised in midair.

Jule looked in dismay at Dorrie.

"He's married a girl from the country," she hurried into the uncomfortable silence. "Mart Brown's girl, you know, from out Mt. Vernon way. A fine little girl, he tells me—a fine little girl."

"Lew Mason," whispered Linda.

Birchfield would know, of course. Whenever she passed the poolroom the men would say: "She lives in the same house with Lew Mason! Trash!"

* * *

Dorrie was up in old man Wickley's room when Lew Mason brought his bride to Aunt Jule's.

Old Wickley, his tangled white beard drooping over the patchwork quilt, was propped up in bed reading aloud from a wonderful book. His immense sonorous voice rolled great boulders around the room. PARMENIDES...ANAXAGORAS...HERACLITUS...EMPEDOCLES ...PROTAGORUS...DEMOCRITUS...Words, names, leaped out of sentences that were too small for them.

"Oh lovely, lovely," breathed Dorrie, her heavy black brows drawn together in ecstatic pain. Mr. Wickley was God, and she was his favorite angel. Only God wouldn't have such a musty room, and the chances were that God would have clean sheets, too.

The old man read with his sunken eyes closed and without turning a page. Dorrie could have read it almost in the same way, because she had heard it so often.

It was generously understood by her grandmother that Dorrie's hours in old Wickley's attic chamber were spent in dusting his books and cleaning things up. In fact, Dorrie always made vague mention of "cleaning up Mr. Wickley's room," but her dustcloth had never desecrated that great black walnut secretary, nor had she ever ventured to collect the books from the chairs, the floor, or the foot of the walnut four-poster bed where Mr. Wickley spent most of his time. Cobwebs collected in the corners or the ceiling and cradled dried flies for years, but Dorrie's eyes never saw them, in spite of her constantly watching blue rose vines wriggle deliriously up a yellow wall to the ceiling. Dorrie saw only an ancient waxen face above a black dressing gown, lean palsied fingers leafing old books, and a long pole of sunlight tipping from the high window down to a certain huge brown carpet rose near Mr. Wickley's bed.

And there was that great voice hurling magnificent words at the walls . . . sometimes the sound of mice squealing and scampering in the eaves overhead.

The first thing that Mr. Wickley had ever said to Dorrie was when she opened his door ten years ago—a somber little gnome in blue calico—

"Child, do you know about the beginning? First there was a crust floating through boundless—"

And Dorrie had obediently pictured a dried bread crust soaring uncertainly among black clouds. But she had listened gravely to the old gentleman ever since. There was glamour about things you didn't understand. And it was better not to know what they meant but to think dreamily about what they ought to mean. You picked out words and played with them . . .

Today Dorrie kept an eye out the window to see what Lew Mason's bride would look like. Oh, wasn't Linda furious! Dorrie didn't intend to leave the haven of the attic room until Linda had gone to the lumber office for the day, because Linda invariably pounced on her younger sister as well as her grandmother when she was in such moods.

"They're here," Dorrie announced aloud, drawing her head back from the window. "Lew's wife has a red hat and a feather fur. Don't I wish I had one?"

Old Wickley continued his reading. The pleasant thing about the friendship of these two was their ability to ignore each other so completely.

"Linda's gone now," pursued Dorrie. "I see her crossing the tracks. Wouldn't she be mad if she knew her petticoat showed? Well, I shan't tell her. Like as not get my head taken off."

She picked up her dustcloth, stage property solely, to be carried about the house every morning and occasionally flourished over a chair if Linda or one's grandmother appeared. She had a fit of conscience now and, going over to the black walnut highboy, dusted with painstaking care the portrait in a wicker frame of a young man—Mr. Wickley's son—wearing a bowler hat, with solemn dignity, over one eye. Her responsibilities thus removed, Dorrie felt free to go downstairs.

Mr. Wickley did not look up as she quietly made her exit. Two words fell into the hall before she closed the door.

"Pythagorous . . . An-ax-im-in-us," she silently repeated and hurried downstairs.

* * *

Lew Mason's bride was thrilled over Aunt Jule's house. She had never been away from the farm before. It was glorious . . . She sat on the table in the summer kitchen adjoining Jule's own kitchen and swung her handsome legs. She glowed, her full red lips parted, as the old woman explained the peculiarities of the gas stove. Her heavy Corylopsis fragrance mingled with the gas and the unmistakable stable odor which Lew freely exuded.

The bridegroom sat in a chair, his fat stolid face fixed blankly on his bride's swinging ankles, his pipe sagging from his mouth. Every now and then he removed the pipe and, aiming for some unknown reason at a very particular spot by the stove, spat.

Lew was forty, and had been dully surprised to find himself married to Mart Brown's daughter. He had gone out to Mart's farm to buy a bay mare, but found the filly on the market as well. She was tall, flashing-eyed, full-bosomed, well-developed at seventeen, wild to be free, and thirsty for life. She was an innocent country lass—but that was solely through lack of opportunity. To be sure, when she was ten or eleven, some boy cousins had spent a summer on the farm, and out in the hayloft they had played fascinating if elemental games. Unfortunately, the boys had left before Esther had mastered quite all of life's mysteries, and she was seventeen before further opportunity, in the person of Lew Mason, presented itself.

Lew was forty and he was fat, but he was a man and, Esther felt, a willing enough coworker in life's laboratory. Lew took two days to buy the mare and wed the filly, but long before he reached Aunt Jule's, he had sold the mare, for the filly was all one man could handle.

"You've got a sweet little wife," Jule turned from the stove to Lew. "You're mighty lucky, Lew Mason. Mighty lucky."

The girl giggled and jumped from the table. Lew merely filled his pipe again and spat.

"This is my little granddaughter," said Jule, catching sight of Dorrie peeping in the doorway. "Dorrie Shirley, my son's youngest girl. She goes to high school, but of course this is her vacation."

"How old are you?" asked the bride, cocking her handsome healthy face to one side and staring at Dorrie.

The bride had high, pointed breasts which stuck out in two great peaks under her tight red sweater.

"Fifteen," said Jule. "She's little, though, like the Marshes. Linda, that's the older girl, takes after the Shirleys and my people. She's eighteen. She's been working in the lumber office, ever since graduation. You and Linda will be great friends."

Dorrie suppressed a cynical smile at this. Linda, who bound a towel tightly over her bosom so there wouldn't be any creases, make friends with a girl who didn't even wear a brassiere!

"You don't keep men here, then?" questioned Esther, with a side glance at her husband.

"Oh, yes, there's old Mr. Wickley, and transients, on and off."

"Crazy Wicky, the townfolks call him," Lew muttered in a weary monotone, "account he don't know nothing but books. He stays up there year in and year out, don't he, Aunt Jule?"

Aunt Jule nodded. She kept one hand on Dorrie's rich brown hair, though Dorrie wiggled a little.

"A fine old gentleman, though, if ever there was one. Yes, indeed, a fine old gentleman. He's from the East, you know."

"The East?" breathed Esther, wide-eyed.

Dorrie yearned to be from the East, so she could see that awe in people's eyes when she told them.

"Good family and all," Jule lowered her voice again. "A scholar and a gentleman."

"No, Grandma," corrected Dorrie, "a gentleman and a scholar is what Grandpa always said."

Jule looked from her granddaughter to Lew and Esther.

"Fancy her remembering," she said absently. For a moment she forgot the young couple waiting before her. Her golden eyes widened and were misted with old memories. She stared out the window, across the garbage-strewn, weedy back garden, her gaze fixed, entranced . . . Clouds of smoke from a passing train floated across the weeds, forming odd shapes . . . A great collie dog leaping up at a big, gray-bearded man, whose leonine gray head was flung back in silent laughter . . .

Dorrie nudged her grandmother. The old woman blinked . . . the collie and his master faded into air . . .

"Three dollars a week," she murmured to the man on the chair. She glanced back wistfully to the ragged garden.

Lew Mason took out a rusty leather wallet and selected three of his seven one-dollar bills to give to Jule.

"I'll be gettin' back to the stable," he said heavily, replacing his wallet in his hip pocket. He blew his nose with unaffected vigor and lumbered out the back screen door. His bride looked after him with a speculative, half-teasing air.

Dorrie felt that Lew should have kissed his wife—after all they'd only been married a little while. Bridegrooms were supposed to be very tender with young brides. Ugh! How awful to be kissed by fat flabby Lew Mason, with his swimming red-rimmed eyes and tobacco-drooling mouth!

"Aunt Jule! Aunt Jule!"

Ella Morris's high-pitched voice came from the hallway outside the dark little bedroom. She wheeled her chair through the bedroom door, pushing it open with her fat, black cane.

"Do you know what I just heard, Aunt Jule?" she called shrilly, guiding her wheelchair through the bedroom portieres into the summer kitchen.

Ella was very dressy today, with a great black maline bow at one side of her neck pinned to her perennial black velvet neckband. Her black, oily hair was done in a firm peak at the top of her head, a tight curl drooping over to one side. Her huge bulbous nose was purple with pink rice powder. She had on the gray taffeta dress that old Mrs. Remer had given her two Christmases ago. Ella really felt it was a little too old for her—after all she was barely thirty-one—but she had brightened it up with a red rosette at the belt and wore it for best. Dorrie wondered why she was dressed up, but remembered then that it was Thursday and Mayor Riggs always called on Thursdays.

"More news, Ella?" asked Aunt Jule, appropriately eager for Ella's daily tidbits.

Ella's filmy eyes paid no heed to Dorrie or the girl in the red hat. She was breathing a little heavily from her haste.

"Why, Mr. Bush was just in and said Lew Mason was married! That filthy old pig! Why, I says, Mr. Bush, I—"

"Sh!—Sh!" Jule sent agonized warning.

"—I don't know who'd have him, I says. Nobody of any account, that's sure. Ella, why not, he says; look at me; I'm as fat as Lew—"

"Ella, can't I—" Jule interrupted, "can't I fix you a cup of coffee? I—"

Ella impatiently brushed the interruption aside. "Yes, I says, but you don't smell like Lew. Well I thought he'd die. Laugh? Well—Ella, he says, you certainly do a man good."

Ella prinked her bow and smiled in pleased reminiscence over her waggery. Esther Mason sat very still, a contemptuous smile etched on her face, but Jule tried to smooth matters, once more.

"What did Mr. Bush say about that new property of his?"

"Do wait till I've finished my story, Aunt Jule. Here's the joke. Mr. Bush said Lew was bringing his wife here to live. Mind you—here! In this house! Well, I said, Mr. Bush, if you think Aunt Jule would take people like that! I know, I says, she takes queer people, but not folks like Lew Mason. Ugh. Why she'd just as soon have Tim Cruger himself! Ha! Ha! Do you think, Mr. Bush, I says, that I could live in the house with Lew Mason and whatever woman he's got? Well, I says, certainly not. Now can you imagine? I'll bet you he's got some bad woman from Mansfield!...Wonder what she looks like."

Jule made an effort to speak but her voice failed her.

Esther Mason walked slowly over to the wheelchair, her hips swaying with insolent rhythm. She pulled the red hat leisurely over one eye and then rested one hand on her hip, her dark eyes scornfully on the cripple.

"Have a look," she said. "I'm Mrs. Lew Mason."

* * *

Linda sometimes allowed her young sister to help her dress on the evenings she was invited out.

Linda's parties were rare, for she refused to mingle with the factory girls who went to Max's Saturday night dances. The nice girls—Gertrude Stall's friends—did not care to adopt Jule's granddaughter into their circle. Since their common school days had ended, they had not even bothered to speak to her, but Linda had made their snobbery easier by her own proud aloofness.

Occasionally she went out for a walk with Mary James, the bookkeeper in the lumber office where Linda worked. Sometimes, as tonight, she went to the parties Mary gave to the Bible class of the Lutheran church. Mary was twenty-five and had frizzed colorless hair and nose glasses. Her father was a miller, well enough off to move in better social circles except that he walked twice a day through Birchfield in a floury suit, with a dinner pail.

The family was certainly not of the town's elect, but Mary's church work gave them respectability at least. That was something.

Linda went upstairs to her room directly after supper, and Dorrie followed her. Linda had had her own room almost as long as Dorrie could remember, holding out stubbornly against Jule's gentle suggestions about sharing it with her sister, or with a very refined lady lodger. It was a very small room, but there was not a moment in the day when it was not immaculate. Linda was conducting a war now with Jule for permission to paint the old black walnut dresser and bed white.

Dorrie thought her sister very lovely. She sat cross-legged on the floor, enchanted, while Linda, slim and straight in her chaste muslin slip and black lisle stockings, combed and recombed her long flaxen hair. Linda had a pair of silk stockings, but she only wore these to the annual alumni dances of the Birchfield High School.

The two girls had little to say to each other, but their silences were precious, since that was all they had ever shared. Linda moved quietly about the room, folding and putting away each garment she removed, with a natural daintiness that fascinated Dorrie.

Dorrie wasn't like that. She liked to have her closet and dresser drawers a mad jumble so that she could be continually astonished to find things she didn't know she owned. That very morning, for instance, she had discovered an old scrap of velvet in the corner of her closet. She had thrust it down her neck and gone about all day feeling its luscious sheen against her skin. She swished her skirts, imagining that her whole dress was velvet, like that small patch. At this very moment she could feel its soft warmth in her bosom.

"Dorrie," Linda said suddenly, "have you been using my lilac toilet water?"

"No," said Dorrie, achieving casualness with remarkable ease. "Is it all gone?"

"Almost. Somebody's used it." Linda allowed the matter to drop for the moment. She sprinkled a few drops on her handkerchief and laid it on the bed beside her leghorn hat and white serge coat.

Dorrie felt relieved. She went to the corner of the room and studied the oval marble-topped table where Linda kept her books. Owen Meredith's *Lucile*, Ella Wheeler Wilcox's *Maurine*, and a Harrison Fisher *Book of Girls*—all commencement presents.

"I'll wash this table for you, Linda," offered Dorrie generously. "It's a little dirty."

"All right," Linda answered, rubbing a chamois over her clear shell-pink cheeks. "Clean the whole room tomorrow if you like."

Dorrie hastily changed the subject.

"Mrs. Stall came to see Ella today," she said. Linda's hand, about to adjust a shoulder strap, paused in midair. Her heart stopped. Stall . . . That name was always in her heart, yet whenever someone spoke it out she was stunned.

"She came in her auto," continued Dorrie, "and she brought Ella a box of peppermints. They're in Ella's bottom drawer."

"Don't you dare to touch them!" Linda said tensely.

She began nervously to draw a ribbon through her embroidered camisole. She was afraid to speak, for she was sure Mrs. Stall's spirit lurked around her door. Mrs. Will Stall, the divinely anointed Mrs. Will Stall, a social leader of Birchfield and mother of Courtenay Stall, the boy who had occupied Linda's whole thought for five years . . .

Dorrie was aware of Linda's feeling about the Stalls. Linda was aghast when Dorrie spoke slightingly of anything—even the awful pink garage of the Stalls. Linda was struck dumb with indignation when Dorrie implied that Courtenay Stall was not a god. Linda was white and wretched all day Sundays after Courtenay Stall had driven past in his car with Lucy Remer or another chosen one. Oh, it was a simple matter to read Linda, Dorrie thought.

"I heard her tell Ella that Courtenay was taking his sister to the country club dance tonight," Dorrie pursued.

Linda, slipping her round white arms into the sleeves of the Alice blue voile, felt an ache of relief. It was easier to bear her exclusion from the Birchfield Country Club and Courtenay's circle if he was merely escorting his own sister. It was the constant picture of him with Lucy Remer, Louise May, and girls like that, not nearly as pretty as herself but graced with proper backgrounds, that tore at Linda's heart.

She adjusted her thick yellow plaits about her face.

"It can't always be this way," she thought. "He will notice me someday. He will see that I am not like the cheap people that live in this house, even if I do stay under the same roof. He will see that I belong at the Birchfield Country Club dances, and on the parties those girls give. And all Birchfield will see it too. They can't—oh, they can't doom me to this forever. They *can't!*"

When that day came, Linda reflected, she would always be polite to Mary James, but she wouldn't go to any more of her Bible class parties. Ah, if tonight she were only going to the country club dance instead of to Mary's! Linda flamed with the injustice of it, an injustice she blamed on Jule and Dorrie and Lew Mason, rather than on the town.

"Why do they call it the country club, Linda?" Dorrie asked idly. "They don't have any clubhouse, and they don't have it in the country. They have their parties in the Elks' Hall, just like Max's Saturday night dances. Almost the same people go, too, except that they pay a dollar instead of a quarter, and old Mr. Remer wears his dress suit . . . Honestly, I don't see why they call it the country club."

Linda was always disgusted with her younger sister's lack of social insight. She turned from her mirror with a shrug of contempt.

"You never see anything," she said coldly. Ah, how fiercely she wished she were going to the country club dance! . . . To dance just once with Courtenay . . . to be seen with him . . . to—merely to watch him! Her desire was anguish to her long desiring heart. She shut her eyes quickly to stop the tears. Linda was not one to weep. Her tears stopped way down and made a sharp chain twisting her heart.

"Well, I don't see what difference the name makes when it's the same thing," insisted Dorrie. Then she added, in fairness, "'Course, they do take the cab to club dances, and walk to Max's; and then they have punch . . . Ella says so. But it seems to me they might just as well call the club dances Max's dances, and Max's dances the club dances. See?"

"Dorrie Shirley!" Linda hoarsely rebuked. Desecration. Sheer desecration. For unlike many social outcasts, Linda refused to comfort herself with cynical reflections on the insignificance of the society that rejected her. The more cruelly society treated her, the more exalted it became in her eyes, and the more desirable became its favor.

Dorrie was silenced. She helped Linda into the white serge coat. Linda turned out the gas and went downstairs. Dorrie meekly followed her, but returned a few minutes after Linda left to hurriedly douse her velvet scrap with Linda's lilac water.

Ella and Jule were sitting on the dark porch as Linda glided quietly across the lawn.

"Oh Linda!" Ella called shrilly, and not without malice, "Going to the country club dance?"

"No!" said Linda savagely.

Under the streetlamp she saw Esther Mason, giggling, insolent, coquetting with two high school boys . . . Revolting! That showed the kind of person she was!

"Hello, Linda Shirley," Esther called out impudently. "Going to the dance?"

Taut with angry humiliation, Linda hurried on, her chin high in the air, her starched petticoats rustling in impotent despair.

* * *

Aunt Jule's house was full of lodgers by the time school began in the fall. The parlor, equipped with a handsome oak folding bed, was turned into a living room for Dick and Marie Farley. Dick used to work in the factory, but he'd gone to New York for a year, and when he came back with his New York bride, they put him out on the road "selling." Dick didn't seem to care what people thought because he put his wife under Aunt Jule's care while he toured the Indiana territory for the Birchfield Soap Company. She wasn't at all snobbish as you'd think a New York girl would be, but she did stay in her room most all the time. Her eyes were always red from weeping. Ella said she supposed she was homesick.

The big north room upstairs was let to an elderly theatrical pair— Mr. and Mrs. Horace Winslow. Their company broke up in Birchfield and the Winslows just stayed. They were as harmless a couple you could find, and there was no reason for Linda's active resentment of their presence in the house, except that Mrs. Winslow did lace and rouge a little. But then Linda hated all stage people.

The Winslows were old troopers, but they were tired of the stage. This last tour had certainly been a lesson to them both! No more stage for the Winslows! They were going to settle right down here in Birchfield. For the time they would stay at Jule's, and they didn't mind eating at Red Turner's shack. But eventually they would have a dear little cottage, and adopt a little girl, and have a canary.

"Horace has never been fond of the stage really," Mrs. Winslow confided to Ella and Jule around the kitchen stove. "He just kept up on my account. And at last the chance has come for him to make his dream come true. No more one-night stands, no more grease paint, no more drafty dressing rooms, no more nasty monkey acts to compete with! Really, it was a wonderful thing for Horace that our show went on the rocks just when it did. He couldn't have endured the life much longer. Horace, you know, is just a plain everyday man—not the least bit theatrical."

Horace, impressive in wing collar, cutaway coat, and iron gray mustachios, took a long walk every day and went to see houses with the real estate agent. He was very courtly and dignified. Aunt Jule was very proud of him. Ella was very careful about her grammar when he was around.

"Alice is not of the stage at all," he told Aunt Jule one evening in low-toned confidence. "If you knew how she has suffered because of my selfish ambitions! A homebody—really, simply a little homebody."

So they looked about for a prospective home, and Mr. Winslow decided to see the principal about teaching English in the high school. Aunt Jule promised to use her influence.

Poor Aunt Jule! As if she had any influence with any of the Birchfield authorities!

Mrs. Winslow's faded violet eyes would blink lovingly upon her majestic spouse at the end of each day's questing.

"There's no hurry, while our savings last," she would murmur. And then—"But it will be sweet to have the little house, Horace. Just to live a sweet, natural life. Oh, Horace!"

"As fine a little couple as you'd ever find," Jule whispered to Dorrie in the intimacy of their bedroom. Dorrie lay in the bed, shading her eyes—golden, like Jule's—with her hand, waiting for her grandmother to finish puttering and come to bed.

"She has pretty clothes," said Dorrie, sociably. "I looked in her trunk, and they're all silk, with brilliants sewed on them and everything. She's fixing one over, and if she doesn't like it she said I could have it. It's pink satin with diamonds embroidered all over, and blue scalloped edges. I hope she gives it to me."

"Well, I think that's mighty sweet of her," Jule declared, much moved. "Too bad Linda couldn't have one too. And they pay their four-fifty every Saturday, just as regular! A lovely couple. I wish Lew Mason would do as much."

"Esther spends all his money," Dorrie said sagaciously. "She buys remnants all the time and makes waists and garters. She's always sewing something like that."

"Nonsense!" scolded Jule. "What would she be making garters for?"

"She said," replied Dorrie, "that everybody was stealing them all the time. I asked her why she didn't have her dresser drawer locked, and she just laughed . . . She waits outside the schoolhouse nights and talks to the boys."

"Hush up and go to sleep," Jule commanded irritably. "I declare, you'd talk all night. All your silly little tattle. You're as bad as Ella."

Her old eyes blinked weakly without her spectacles. She pinned her thick muslin gown at the throat, dropped her teeth with a cheerful little click in the glass of water on the table, and turned out the gas. She climbed heavily into bed beside Dorrie's warm little figure, and the next moment the young girl was listening with fascinated pleasure to the old woman's peculiar snore: Um-m-m-pah-pah-s-s-ss tck-tck . . . um-m-m-pah-pah-s-s-ss-tck-tck . . .

* * *

Uncle Theodore and Aunt Laura came to Birchfield in October. Theodore was Jule's oldest son. Laura was her only daughter. Jule would have given up both of them for Jerry, the father of Dorrie and Linda.

Uncle Theo and Aunt Laura had each married well years ago while their father still lived. People came from far and wide to talk to old Judge Shirley on his farm, and Laura had been won by one visitor, a young Columbus lawyer. Theo had gone to Columbus later and had small difficulty in selecting a suitably wealthy and aristocratic wife from among the Columbus best people. Jule was only the handsome wife of Judge Shirley, then . . . Her children had not thought of her as a future menace to their social standing. But now . . .

During the eighteen years that Jule had been living her life in her own way, beyond the Birchfield railroad station, her two children had come to her at intervals to try and persuade her to give up her chosen career. She could come and live with them . . . She could go and live with Aunt Eleanor in California and they would send her an allowance . . . Anything but this degrading rooming house!

They had long ceased to bring their families on these annual pilgrimages, for Jule betrayed the most astounding indifference to Theo's two spindly, well-bred children and Laura's Margaret. She was unfailingly rude to Laura's husband and insulting to Theo's cultured wife. After a time, the brother and sister came alone to Birchfield and endeavored fussily to readjust the tranquil routine of their unnatural mother's life.

Linda alone adored her Aunt Laura, but both Laura and Theo were too resentful of their mother's partiality for Jerry's children to show any affection for their young nieces. Linda wished sometimes that they would invite her to Columbus and take her away forever from the misery of this sordid boarding house. But in her heart Linda knew that she could not leave Courtenay Stall . . . You never won battles by running away from the field. In Columbus she might benefit by her aunt's prestige, but what good would it do her if Courtenay, back in Birchfield, didn't know about the change? He might even marry while she was gone . . . Perhaps, Linda thought, it was just as well Aunt Laura didn't invite her.

Uncle Theo was slight, sharp-faced, and old-maidish-looking. He wore nose spectacles with a black ribbon, for he was a lawyer. He had a sandy Vandyke beard and a nervous, distracted manner. He hoped people would not forget what great things were weighing on his mind . . . Jule had never forgiven him for not looking like his father. The good-for-nothing Jerry had been the exact picture of Judge Shirley . . . The magnificent frame, the splendid head, the grave eyes that concealed constant laughter . . . It was easy to forgive Jerry for being lazy and indolent.

Aunt Laura bore an outward resemblance to her mother, but her chin was much stronger, and her eyes were gray and cold. She wore earrings and expensive furs now that Richard Tooley, her husband, was a corporation lawyer. She twisted a long chain of beaten gold, which hung over her coat.

Linda had stayed home from work the afternoon they came and sat close to her aunt, admiring the expensive perfection of her blue broadcloth suit. If only the town would judge her by her Columbus relatives instead of by her grandmother!

"Mother, do you allow that child to paint her face?" accused Laura, pointing a horrified finger at Dorrie's cheeks.

Dorrie, who had been sitting on the footstool, studying her relatives under calculating black brows, suddenly began to wiggle. Her grandmother looked at her oddly. That very morning she had had a vague impression that Dorrie was rubbing red crepe paper on her face. It had not troubled her especially. Dorrie was always up to something like that.

"Dorrie's very healthy," she said placidly. "Her cheeks are always rosy."

Linda blushed with shame. Dorrie twisted her handkerchief. Uncle Theo looked quite disgusted, and Aunt Laura pursed her lips in repressed annoyance. "I do wish you'd give up this awful place, Mother," she went on. "Each time we come you have worse people living here. That livery stable man and that wife of his! She's a hussy, you can see. Mother, if you'd only realize how hard it is for Theo and me, when any of our friends come to Birchfield and see—all this." She dabbed a handkerchief at her eyes. "One's mother the town character, and her house the most talked-of place in the whole country. Actually, when we got off the train, the brakeman was telling some frightful looking creature to go to Aunt Jule's across the way if he wanted a good place to stay!"

Uncle Theo coughed and adjusted his tiepin with nervous fingers.

"Berenice absolutely refuses to come up here anymore," he said, in his quick jerky voice. "And you know you ought to have a little consideration for Father. If he had ever guessed you would do such a thing, he would turn in his grave. How he would have suffered! Really, Mother . . ."

Jule sat in the carpet-seated rocker and crocheted. She loved the whole world, but she had not the faintest spark of maternal feeling for her two oldest children. They were wealthy and established and dull, and Jule had no use for such people, even when they were of her own blood. Now, Jerry—dear, tattered, irresponsible Jerry! . . . ah, Jerry, was her son!

"Do you hear from Jerry, Mother?" asked Aunt Laura.

Jule nodded enigmatically.

"Does he send you money for the girls' support?" demanded Uncle Theo, nodding toward Dorrie and Linda.

"Yes," lied Jule. "Every month."

Theo and Laura looked unconvinced.

"I'd send you something, you know—a few dollars now and then," Theo said, in his nervous, fretful way. "Only there's no reason why I should be supporting Jerry's children. That's what it amounts to. As for that, you have no right to spend your own good money on them. If Jerry ignores his responsibilities, they don't fall to you. After all, your duty is to your own children."

"Is it?" said Jule tranquilly, the lace edging slipping through her deft fingers. "Well, it may seem funny but the only one of you I ever had any use for was Jerry. Then he ran away—but—but of course I know where he is. I'm expecting him back any day now. He—he's gotten interested in oil."

Aunt Laura made an inarticulate exclamation.

"Talk about being ashamed of me," Jule went on, with rising annoyance. "Laura, there, was such an ugly baby I used to make Mrs. Durkin wheel her out all the time for fear people would think she was mine."

Jule emitted a chuckle of triumph. She got up and started toward the kitchen, pretending to have important matters awaiting her personal attention.

"Sorry you folks can't stay for supper," she said blandly. "Your train goes at 4:40, so maybe you'd better be going. I'll say goodbye now—have to fix a room upstairs for the man the brakeman sent over. He's a molder by trade. This is their bad season, and he's working his way to Akron to the rubber works."

Aunt Laura and Uncle Theo sat in thwarted indignation for a few minutes after their mother disappeared. Aunt Laura's face was quite red.

"Linda," she said in a controlled voice, "how is Mother's health? Do you think she is quite well?"

"Oh, yes," Linda assured her.

Aunt Laura thought unwillingly how pretty Linda had become, so fair and slim . . . Margaret *would* eat pastry, though; and the child couldn't help her teeth. At least she was an heiress and a Tooley, and those things counted more for a girl than good looks. It was like Jerry to have a beautiful daughter, though. Things always had come to him. She and Theo always got the worst of things . . .

"I wish she'd talk sense," Uncle Theo grumbled, tapping the red roses on the carpet with his umbrella. "Laura and I made this trip especially to discuss with her where she'd like to be buried—at Caledonia, with father, or in the old Marsh lot in Circleville."

"Is she going to be buried?" asked Dorrie, bewilderedly.

Dorrie was terribly stupid about some things, Aunt Laura thought.

"Eventually, of course," she snapped. "After all, your grandmother is close to seventy, you know."

"I don't think she'll die," said Dorrie comfortably.

"Never mind." Uncle Theo's tone was cold. He was not interested in children. When they were other people's, they were bound to be badly behaved, and when they were your own, they were bound to have adenoids or chickenpox or something.

He nodded briefly to his sister. She drew on her gloves with a sigh of resignation. Their visits always ended like this.

Linda watched enviously. She had been waiting for a good chance to tell her aunt that she could wear her cast-off clothes and that she was pretty good at fixing things over.

"What a pretty suit, Aunt Laura," she said shyly.

"You shall have it next year," said her aunt, with a smile of restrained sweetness.

"It will look wonderful on Linda," Dorrie vouchsafed pleasantly. "It's too young for you, Aunt Laura."

She was a little hurt, then, because Linda alone was asked to accompany her relatives to the station. She watched them from the doorway, absently wiping her rosy cheeks on Linda's white silk scarf.

* * *

Dorrie always walked home from school with Phil Lancer. Phil was stout and fair and constantly dumbfounded by Dorrie's cleverness. He lived on the wrong side of the railroad track, too, and so he was not—at least for a long time—conscious of the Birchfield feeling about the Shirley girls. He and Dorrie had been playmates since the first grade. From that year on, Dorrie had done all his lessons for him. In English VII he was asked sometimes to read his themes aloud, and the stupid boy could never pronounce half the words Dorrie had put into them.

"There's going to be a hayride party tonight," Phil said one evening on the way home. He played football after school now and only came home with Dorrie once a week.

"What of it?" answered Dorrie pertly. She never was asked to any of the parties. Phil, either, so far as she knew.

"Wondered if you were going," said Phil languidly. Playing on the team had subtly changed Phil's social position. Dorrie didn't realize. "Thought I'd go."

"Oh," said Dorrie, quite shocked. And again, "Oh!"

He would go to parties now and maybe get a crush on Molly Miller or some of those "nice" girls from East Walnut Street. Dorrie felt lonesome already. What would she do without Phil? Gracious! She slipped her hands into her sweater pockets.

"Hope you have a good time," she said jauntily.

"Oh, I don't care," said Phil, who was secretly well pleased at his sudden acceptance in the right circle. He had never had the ambition to seek it before, but now that he was wearing long pants and silk ties, he saw things a lot differently. A fellow really had to be careful whom he ran around with.

Dorrie shot a covert look at her erstwhile boon companion. He was much nicer, she reflected, when he was seven. Such a shy, dreamy little fellow. They used to hunt moles' nests in his father's wheat fields, and they had gathered Johnny-jump-ups and boysand-girls and ferns every May Day. And in fall they had raked leaves and made maple chains. They had built bonfires in Jule's front yard, and Jule had called them into the kitchen for cookies and milk . . . He had been such a shy little boy. But the shyness had settled into surliness, and the dreaminess was sheer stupidity. Phil Lancer was growing up to be a good Birchfield citizen.

They walked a little slower down Walnut Street. Phil was unwilling to speak of anything but his society debut, and Dorrie for her part was determined to betray no interest.

"They say they play all sorts of kissing games," she said detachedly. "Those girls are like that."

"Hmm," Phil commented. He lit a cigarette. He had just learned to smoke this fall, but maybe after a while you get used to it. "The party's to end up at Molly Miller's. They've got eleven rooms in their house. Gee, I'll bet her old man's rich."

"She's got a goiter," said Dorrie frankly.

Phil began to whistle. Along the wide street, with its rows of neat little houses set in great lawns, they were the only pedestrians. From one of the houses issued a spirited attempt at the "Scarf Dance" on a Story & Clark piano. It would be followed, Dorrie knew, by "Meditation," "Star of the East," and, if the listeners were willing, "The Midnight Fire Alarm." Of course it was Miss Lundquist, the leading music teacher, out giving samples of her work in homes recently visited by pianos. When a pupil was captured, she was promised that identical repertoire within the next two terms. Presently, the faded little woman in her brown velvet suit would emerge and cross the street to another house. A pleased housewife would hastily cast aside her apron and welcome the harbinger of art into the darkened parlor. The piano would be unveiled. Miss Lundquist would ask for a basin of hot water to warm her cold hands. The "Scarf Dance" would begin.

"Do you think you could give Bertha a piece where she could cross her hands?" the prospective client would inquire. "I saw you let Gertrude Stall play one at your last recital."

Phil nodded toward the house now bursting with "The Midnight Fire Alarm."

"Molly Miller takes lessons from her," he said, with a pride in Molly's accomplishment that alarmed Dorrie.

"She isn't as good a teacher as Miss Bellows at our house," said Dorrie contrarily. She loathed Molly Miller, suddenly. "Only Gertrude Stall takes of Miss Lundquist, and that makes her the best. Gee! I'll bet if Miss Bellows's folks hadn't lived on a dirt road and gone to the frame church, she would have had better luck. Maybe your Molly would have taken of her then."

"She isn't my Molly," said Phillip.

"You wish she was," taunted Dorrie.

From one of the houses—the pink one with the big porch and the porte cochere—Molly Miller herself emerged with another girl. They had tennis rackets. They skipped down the front steps and stopped short in front of Phil and Dorrie.

"Hello, Phil," said Molly Miller, her brown eyes sweeping Dorrie from head to foot with a certain subtle amusement.

Phil mumbled something, his face a fiery red. Dorrie returned Molly's stare with bland interest. But when the girls had passed, she heard them tittering.

"Did you ever see anything like it? . . ."

And the other girl's voice, muffled with laughter. "One day in English her face was rouged! I . . ."

Dorrie knit her brows in bewildered surprise. It must be they meant her. She felt hot and sick inside. She glanced at Phil. He was still very red and looking intently at the sidewalk. Dorrie saw Linda coming out of the lumber office on the corner.

"Come on," she urged Phil. "Let's catch up with Linda."

But Phil, red and inarticulate, was striding across the street to the poolroom, waving to some invisible friend.

"Where did you get that awful dress?" demanded Linda as soon as she caught sight of her younger sister. "What does Grandma mean letting you wear such horrible things?"

Dorrie looked down at the fetching little school dress Jule had made her from Mrs. Winslow's pink satin. She had been so gloriously happy in it, swishing down the aisles in the schoolroom, astounding the teachers and all the other girls.

"I—I like it," she said.

"Anything but filthy dirty satin," exploded Linda. "And I suppose you showed yourself to the whole town. Come on home. I'm going to make Grandma use some sense about your clothes. It's enough to make you the laughingstock of the whole town."

Dorrie exclaimed in sudden understanding. She looked over her shoulder at the two girls in white, swinging their tennis rackets far down the street. So that was why they had laughed?

"I don't care," she said, winking back her tears defiantly. "Jealous, that's what they are—just jealous."

Chapter Two

Linda said nothing that night about her sister's wardrobe because Marie Farley was in the kitchen with Jule, and Linda was a little afraid of Marie. Marie was from New York, and while to Birchfield, New York was as meaningless and remote as a billion dollars—Akron or even Mansfield meaning far more to them as a symbol of culture—still, New York was East, and, as East, Birchfield bowed to it.

Marie was not pretty. She was slight and flat-breasted, and her nose was long. She had chic, however, and Linda appreciated it without understanding what it was. Marie's sleeves were skin-tight, and her hair was always perfect. She always wore silk stockings and French heels and she had very broad A's. She had met Dick in New York and married him only a few months ago. Now she stayed at Aunt Jule's, waiting for Dick's weekend at home and sobbing all night for her lost paradise.

"I was afraid in my room, so I came down," she told Linda when the two sisters came in. "I could hear Mr. Mason, underneath, beating his wife. I'm sure he was beating her. It was terrible."

"Oh, no," said Jule, her golden eyes clouded. She was rolling out a pie crust on the kitchen table. "I don't think Lew Mason's like that."

"She deserves it," piped up Ella Morris, suddenly wheeling into the room, dressed in her red serge for the mayor's call. "That girl's been going out with other men. Staying out. Why, Will Stall says to me, you've got a vampire in your house, Ella Morris. I says, if you mean that Mason girl, Will Stall, I says, she's worse than that. Going around with little high school boys. Still, I says, I have men of all ages calling on me, keeping me up half the night, so I suppose you think I'm a vampire too. Well, you are at that, he says, and I wish you could have heard us laugh."

Laughing with Mr. Stall! Linda quivered.

"Mrs. Winslow says Esther ought to go on the stage," said Dorrie. "She has such a fine figure."

"Mrs. Winslow!" sniffed Linda.

"A fine little lady," said Jule mechanically. She popped the pie into the oven and wiped her flushed face. She was not good at arguments. All she could do was to repeat her defense of whatever soul was being accused. People were so unreasonable.

"I was sure they were fighting," said Marie, apologetically.

Linda sat down wearily in a chair. Coming home was always like this—more shame—always. She made a gesture of revolt.

"I'll tell them to leave, I will!" she said shrilly. "I don't see why Grandma keeps them. I'll go in now—"

Before Jule could stop her, she had gone over to the summer kitchen and pushed open the door. The women in the big kitchen realized suddenly that it had been silent in the Mason quarters for several minutes. Linda was back as quickly as she had gone. Her face looked oddly baffled.

"She—" she said in a flat voice, "she was sitting on his lap. On his lap . . . They didn't see me."

Jule's face lifted gloriously.

"Just see that," she exclaimed. "That shows."

Linda was silent.

Ella Morris chewed peppermints from a paper bag. Marie Farley smiled a little wry smile at Dorrie, and Dorrie smiled back.

* * *

Later, Marie beckoned impulsively to Dorrie. "Will you go to the bakery and get me a chocolate éclair?" she whispered, fishing in her little mesh bag for her change purse.

Dorrie was flattered at Marie's asking a favor.

"A what?"

"A chocolate éclair."

Dorrie's brow puckered. She went uncertainly out. In a little while she came back empty-handed. No one had ever heard of a chocolate éclair. The baker had laughed, the confectioner had howled, the grocer had promised to tell the joke at lodge that night. A chocolate éclair for the young lady from New York. Like as not she was just trying to show off. Anyway, it was a good joke—and one on New York, too, for some subtle reason.

"They didn't know what it was," reported Dorrie, regretfully.

Whereat, quite unexpectedly, Marie Farley burst into tears.

"This damn town—oh, this damn town!" she wept, passionately. "Oh, Dick, Dick, why did you ever leave me here?"

Linda awkwardly attempted to console her. She led her back to her own room.

Dorrie looked sorrowfully after Marie. It was too bad she couldn't have that thing. What was a chocolate éclair, anyway?

Jule brushed aside two precious tears—one for Esther Mason and one for Marie. Another welled slowly to the tips of her lashes. Perhaps it was for Linda.

Ella rattled her bag and munched another peppermint thoughtfully.

"Probably going to have a baby," she observed. "They always get wrought up over nothin' then."

* * *

Esther Mason was drunk with love of the city.

After seventeen years on a farm, Birchfield was Paris to her. Wine was in her veins, delight was in her body. Lew brushed only vaguely the fringes of her joy.

Lew was away for days at a stretch, buying horses and going to races. Esther thought of him as a satisfactory enough husband. She would always love him for bringing her to the city. When she lay in a damp clump of weeds in some boy's arms, she looked up at the lovely moon and was grateful to Lew for opening the gates to paradise. When she sat on the schoolhouse steps long after midnight, pressed hotly against some man's moist breast, she thought of how much she owed to her husband. When she raced along Maple Avenue at night as the lights came on, she throbbed with gratitude to the man who had given her—the city.

Ah—the city!

The haunting allure of Main Street at dark, with its dim streetlamps and whirring automobiles . . . Glimpses of a strange fair man at the wheel of a roadster passing by . . . men, knowing-eyed men, bending over pool tables in a blue fog of cigarette smoke . . . ragtime airs tinkling shrilly from some porch gramophone . . . creakings of vine-shaded porch swings . . . glowing of cigarette ends on hushed dark side streets . . . breath of stale beer and jangle of men's voices from corner saloons . . .

On hot summer nights, one caught the sense-maddening odor of tobacco smoke and masculine sweat when one passed close by a man.

Ah, the city!

On Wednesday nights the band played in the park and one saw new faces. Twice Esther had seen automobiles with insolent young men exuding a delirious fragrance of whisky and tobacco and Sen-Sen . . . Farm men smelt of cows and hay . . . Lew smelt of stables, and sometimes that, too, intoxicated Esther. But city men! . . .

Esther asked Linda to go to the last of the season's band concerts. She was constantly making overtures to Linda—whether out of ghoulish insolence or sincere admiration it was hard to say. Linda always preserved a frigid restraint.

"I never go to band concerts," said Linda, coldly.

"Let me go!" Dorrie eagerly cried. She had been writing a long epic poem on a roll of old frayed shelf paper, but she much preferred the thrill of a band concert to an artistic triumph.

Esther didn't mind, so Dorrie hurried upstairs and unostentatiously borrowed Linda's red beads and bar pin and pink powder. She rushed after Esther—the back way of course, so that Linda's keen eyes could not suspect the stolen treasures.

Jule washed the dishes. She had called Linda to help her, but Linda, out on the dark porch, had refused to answer. She was nursing the hurt that came when Courtenay Stall's car flew by with a girl in it—a visitor from Lima . . . Courtenay always prided himself on the number of towns in which he had feminine contacts.

Barely an hour after Esther and Dorrie had left, Aunt Jule, rocking in the kitchen in the darkness, saw Dorrie's small white face pressed against the screen door.

"Where's Linda?" she hissed.

Jule nodded toward the front porch, and, reassured, Dorrie came into the room, the beads and bar pin hidden in her pocket in case of an unwelcome encounter.

"Esther went for a ride," she whispered. "Two men in a Chicago Junction automobile called something, and she started joking with them, and then pretty soon she got in. I said I'd come too, only they didn't ask me. Then they went off. Esther said to tell Lew she'd gone to the public library if he came in."

Aunt Jule frowned.

"Hush up, now," she said exasperatedly. "I declare, I never heard a child talk so. And don't let me catch you telling Linda or Ella such tales. The idea!"

Dorrie, somewhat bewildered, tiptoed up to Linda's room to replace the borrowed jewelry.

* * *

Esther came home the next noon in excellent spirits, if a trifle subdued. She put on her apron at once and began frying steak and onions for Lew's noonday meal, calling to Jule now and then from her kitchen. She explained casually how she had run into her father the night before and gone out to the farm all night. Her folks, she said with a self-conscious laugh, felt very badly because she didn't come home oftener.

"I wish you'd brought me some of your father's apples," said Aunt Jule, ignoring Dorrie's suppressed excitement and signals. "I want to put up some jelly. What did he say about fruit this year?"

"He said berries had been pretty poor, except for red raspberries," obliged Esther, stirring her onions industriously. "But he said to tell you that you could have all the apples you needed, because they're better than they've been for five years."

Jule met Dorrie's eye coldly and nodded in quiet triumph.

"I guess little girls see a lot more than what's before their eyes," she rebuked in a low tone.

"But Grandma—those men—"

"What did you say about your eyes, Aunt Jule? I didn't hear," called Esther.

"I was talking to Dorrie," explained Jule. She padded softly across the room into Esther's kitchen. "Ella—" she jerked her head toward the invalid's door and lowered her voice, "—tried to tell me a lot of nonsense about you and some men. Why, I says, the idea! Seems that old Mr. Stall told her. And Mr. Tompkins, too. He came in while I was in her room, and I just up and said to him: 'Mr. Tompkins, I just ran in to tell Ella here what a fine little wife Lew Mason has. She's a mighty fine little woman,' I says."

Esther laughed, reddening a little.

"You're a good pal, Aunt Jule," she declared. "Some of these old hens make me sick with their cackle. 'Taint a girl's fault if the fellows keep after her."

Just then the door opened and Lew Mason came in. Seeing his face, Jule quietly hustled Dorrie back into their own kitchen and closed the door behind her on the happy pair.

* * *

Mr. Winslow was not able to get the high school position after all. Mr. Gaige, the principal, said he had a young lady from Wooster for the place, and besides, he was distrustful of these teachers from foreign universities. (Mr. Winslow's year touring the English provinces had developed into an Oxford degree.) After a while, a position as drugstore clerk opened up, and in view of their decreasing capital, Mr. Winslow accepted it at fifteen dollars a week. "It's so much sweeter this way," Mrs. Winslow told Aunt Jule as they did their ironing together in the kitchen, Dorrie dreamily scouring silverware over on the dining table. "We're not really theatrical at all. At least Horace isn't. Horace feels so deeply for the dear natural things in life. And I'd be the last one to let my ambition come between us. After all, it is a hard life, particularly for a man of Horace's delicate sensibilities . . . It was fate that made our company go on the rocks in this sweet little village. The ideal place for a home."

"Isn't that true!" Jule marveled. "Some say Birchfield's nothing but a dirty little railroad town, but to my mind it's one of the prettiest little cities in Ohio. Ideal for a home. And such lovely people. I tell you, Mrs. Winslow, you couldn't have picked a better place to settle down in."

"I'd rather go on the stage and travel all around," observed Dorrie candidly.

Mrs. Winslow smiled tolerantly over Dorrie's head at Aunt Jule. Then she set the iron carefully down on Mr. Winslow's pink and lavender striped shirt.

"It won't be long before we will find a dear little home," she said gaily. "How happy Horace will be. And, after all, the drugstore is very refined. I was telling Horace only last night, I really think there is a future in it . . . How good you have been to us, Aunt Jule!"

Jule wiped her eyes sentimentally. She was invariably more touched by pseudo emotions than by real ones. She thought Mrs. Winslow was a sweet little woman. She ached when Linda said she dyed her hair and had smelly clothes.

Dorrie was always thrilled when there were actors in the house. She did think, though, that there was something a little odd about the Winslows. Why should Mr. Winslow give her secret instructions to save any mail that came for him and give it to him privately? It was particularly puzzling because Mrs. Winslow had, with some embarrassment, made the same request about any mail that came for her.

"I'd rather Horace didn't see it," she had said.

"They're just actors," Linda said when Dorrie confided this odd coincidence. "Actors are like that. I knew they were no good as soon as Grandma took them. Pretending to be such a devoted couple, and then getting mail on the sly and keeping it a secret from each other! Such trash!"

Dorrie, to solve the mystery, did not hesitate to study the mail that came for the pair. But nothing ever came for them but magazines. The one that she gave with such secrecy to Mr. Winslow was called *Variety*. The one that came for Mrs. Winslow was the *Clipper*. Nothing to make so much fuss over, Dorrie thought.

* * *

Mrs. Winslow was a great comfort to Marie Farley. Mrs. Winslow had been in New York—had, in fact, lived there a whole year—and even though it had been at a period of which Marie had not the slightest recollection, she seized upon the old actress as a long-lost sister.

"It's wonderful to see someone from home again!" she exclaimed. Then she asked eagerly: "Do you know Rector's—and Little Hungary—and Lo Sing's down in Chinatown? Oh, what wonderful times I've had in those places!"

"I'm afraid I didn't do much of that," Mrs. Winslow said, her blue eyes darkening a little with the memory of a starving twelvemonth in an Eighth Avenue rooming house. Six days without so much as a cracker! And Horace, staggering to rehearsals with pneumonia hanging over him! And the frenzied searchings through trunk after trunk for something else to take to the pawn shop! And that cold November night on a Bryant Park bench, Horace's head in her lap . . . her eyes smarting in an agony of tears unshed so that Horace wouldn't see how discouraged she was . . . The mirage of triumph hanging sometimes so near . . . "Dear old New York," Mrs. Winslow sighed. "We were working so hard, you see," she went on, "we didn't get a chance to go out much. Horace and I never really liked New York. That was the year I saw that stage life was too much for Horace."

Marie was disappointed. She dropped back listlessly. Mrs. Winslow knew New York, and yet she was not in love with it. She had been there a whole year, and yet had been glad to leave it. It was incredible. Marie was not sorry when Dorrie came to her door and beckoned mysteriously to Mrs. Winslow. The lady rose alertly and hurried out.

"She wouldn't appreciate New York anyway." Marie turned to Linda. "Actresses never can see anything in a town but billboards and managers."

"I was surprised that you were interested in her," Linda observed. She liked Marie Farley. Marie was only a few years older than she, and her quiet reserve appealed to Linda. True, she was a little queer. Imagine going to the Birchfield House and asking for a lobster salad! Or sending out for chocolate éclairs! Like the rest of Birchfield, Linda felt a superior amusement at such absurd conduct.

"You're not going to stay here all your life, are you, Linda?" questioned Marie.

Linda studied her slim white hands hesitatingly. She had never actually told anyone about Courtenay—the way she felt about him. Marie was discreet and would sympathize. What a relief to yield a little of her secret to someone!

"I—you see, there's someone here I like," she confessed and at once felt herself lifted out of her dark loneliness. "He doesn't notice me at all, but it can't always be that way. If a girl is good and clean, a man can't blame her because her grandmother's rooming house has a bad name."

Marie looked surprised.

"If I wait long enough, he'll get to know me and perhaps marry me. It's silly to say that, but somehow I've always felt—well, it might happen—and we could live here—"

"My dear, don't!" Marie clasped her hands imploringly. "Don't marry anyone here. I can't bear to think of any other young person being thrust for life into this ghastly hole."

"You mean Grandmother's—"

"No, no!" Marie impatiently interrupted. "Thank heaven for Aunt Jule's! What if Dick had left me at that horrible Mrs. White's!"

She shuddered.

"You don't mean you'd rather stay here than at Mrs. White's?" Linda gasped. Why, Mrs. White had all the nice Birchfield people who boarded. And she moved in circles herself!

"My dear—naturally! Aunt Jule's might be anywhere, but Mrs. White's could never be any place but in Birchfield. Nasty little small-town boarding house!"

Linda was silent from sheer incredulity.

"Why don't you get away while you're still young," Marie suggested, tensely. "Go to New York, Linda, or even Cleveland. Don't get sunk here before it's too late. Married to that ignorant boy—"

"Courtenay's been to Purdue!" Marie laughed convulsively. "Whatever Purdue may be . . . All right, marry him. Go to Columbus once every two years for your winter coat, and Cedar Point every Labor Day . . . Two babies . . . A gramophone . . . and if you really do get cultured enough, there's the Browning Club and a yearly paper comparing Keats with Longfellow. Oh, my dear—my dear!"

Linda arose and looked with cold eyes at Marie.

"If that's the way you feel," she said, "you shouldn't have married a Birchfield man. I'm sure I don't see why you did."

She went out. After that day she was very remote to Marie. There was no use trying to do anything with the girl. She'd never get taken up in Birchfield if she acted that way. Lobsters and éclairs and—what nonsense!

Dorrie often heard Marie sobbing at night in her room. Once, Dorrie couldn't stand it any longer and crawled out of bed. She pattered into the parlor—now the Parleys' bedroom. Marie was sitting up in a rocker, her arms dangling loosely at her sides, her head drooping backward. Her mouth hung partly open as if she no longer had the strength to close it, and tears ran down her still white face. It was as if her tired body were being drained of a colossal despair. Tears flowed, yet the muscles of her face did not even contract. Sobs came from her mouth, yet her lips never moved, for the sounds came from deep down in her body.

Dorrie stood in the doorway, clutching her nightgown, uncertain how to comfort her.

"Marie, I'm here," she said, finally, in a small voice.

Marie's sobbing gradually died away. She opened her eyes drearily. Dorrie poured her a drink of water from the pitcher on the table.

"Wouldn't it be nice," she offered shyly, "if you had a chocolate éclair now?"

Marie's mouth twisted at one corner.

"What a funny child you are, Dorrie," she said in a tired wan voice. "A chocolate éclair isn't what I want now. I want a Bronx cocktail."

Dorrie sat down on the bed, her black-fringed golden eyes fixed on Marie.

"What's New York like, Marie?" she asked softly. "What makes people talk about it—well—the way you do . . . as if it was the end of the world?"

"New York?" Marie closed her eyes and the dear picture flitted tantalizingly across her mind. The eternal jeweled parade to hidden music . . . limousines . . . silken women with souls of fabric . . . grilled iron doors swinging open on costly streets, spilling the fragrance of an old aristocracy . . . a lamplit table in a restaurant . . . enchanting vistas of shop tables piled with rainbow chiffons and velvets . . . the breathless glimpses of unknown worlds, of incredible splendors. . .

There was Dick Farley . . . Marie remembered their mad dancing courtship, whirling through cabarets and theaters and taxicabs . . . hadn't thought of him as being apart from New York. Then, after the wedding, and when he had changed his job . . . Marie winced.

"Dorrie, darling," she said, after a while, "look where love is leading before you follow it . . . People like you and me need something else. All the love in the world can't make up for Birchfield."

Dorrie was silent. Love was love, or else it wasn't, she thought. If it wasn't really love, why, then of course it couldn't make up for things.

"When Dick comes back, and you have your own house, it will be different," she finally consoled Marie. "You'll forget all about New York."

"That's what I'm afraid of," whispered Marie.

She hid her face in her hands. Dorrie, bewildered but sympathetic, stroked the dark hair. Then she tiptoed back to bed. She thought she might write a poem about New York in the morning—the city that made people so unhappy. Someday she would go there, and find out what it was.

* * *

Mr. Wickley wasn't feeling well lately.

No wonder, either, Ella Morris commented to Aunt Jule, for the man ate hardly a morsel of food. Tea and crackers, tea and crackers, a bag of stale pretzels, and some shriveled apricots . . . Nobody could live on that.

And he persistently returned the trays Jule sent up, with hardly a mouthful touched.

Dorrie stayed home from school, one day, to nurse him. It was during examinations, and she felt that her place was at home. She was genuinely fond of the old man, and he liked having her around, even though her boasted "nursing" consisted only of sitting on the window seat, hugging her knees, and dreaming.

Mr. Wickley's face was more parched and yellow than ever, and his old eyes seemed to have sunk deeper into their shadowy sockets. His fingers shook plainly as they leafed over his beloved books, and his voice was strangely hollow. He wasn't really sick, Dorrie thought, he was just old. She suspected that he rather wanted to die, anyway. He had written a letter this afternoon—the first letter Dorrie had ever seen him write, and she was to mail it later on. It was addressed to Roger Wickley III at Harvard University, Cambridge, Mass.

"It must be his grandson," deduced Dorrie. She was familiar enough with the daguerreotype in the wicker frame. That was Roger II, Wickley's son, and he was dead. He was, in the picture, a solemn young man with a thick waxed moustache and a checkered jacket, buttoned at the top but open below to reveal a white waistcoat. His face was long, like Mr. Wickley's, and rose out of a high wing collar up to the derby hat. A hand was thrust into the waistcoat with an air of resolute jauntiness.

"I wonder if the grandson looks like that," meditated Dorrie, sincerely hoping that he didn't. She made a momentary flight to Cambridge and walked majestically across the campus with a young man in a checkered suit and a brown derby set album style on one eyebrow.

No, that would be too bad. She swiftly constructed a Roger III of godlike beauty, who wore evening clothes at all times and was very fond of Shelley. Someday he would come to visit his grandfather, and he would stagger back when he saw Dorrie, and say, "Am I dreaming? At last, the woman I have been seeking all these years!"

Dorrie sighed rapturously. It was sweet of Mr. Wickley to have a grandson like that. She would be very kind to the old man, always, on that account.

"Fire . . . Water . . . Fire . . . Water. . ."

Dorrie's thoughts danced a grave gavotte to the beat of old Wickley's faltering voice.

"Fire . . . Water . . . Fire . . . Water . . ."

"Isn't it lovely," mused Dorrie, "for things not to mean anything?"

What was a "wet soul," she wondered, and why was it best to have a dry one? Sometimes she looked in those strange books Mr. Wickley read from, but the words meant even less in black and white than when rolled from the old man's tongue. She doubted if anybody knew what they were all about. It didn't matter, anyway.

She decided to ask Mr. Wickley outright about his grandson.

"Mr. Wickley, why doesn't your grandson from Harvard come and see you?" she interrupted. "Have you ever seen him? . . . Did you have a terrible quarrel with your family, Mr. Wickley, and is that why you've lived alone all these years?"

"Fire . . . Water . . . Fire . . . Water . . . Being is everything . . . the one reality . . ."

The old man went right on reading . . .

Looking out the window Dorrie could see her grandmother in her gray percale, a white shawl thrown over her head, talking to Tim Cruger in the front yard.

Tim was always drunk, and his clothes were caked with mud from the alleys he had slept in. He had a red, boiled face and slippery blue eyes. When he was particularly drunk he referred to himself as a gentleman and a scholar, and he usually called on Aunt Jule to have this claim verified.

"She's telling him that she thinks he's one of the finest boys in Birchfield," thought Dorrie, catching the earnest tone in Jule's voice, "and he's saying that she's his best friend and there's nobody else in town he'd be willing to take money from, but if she could lend him a quarter, he'd certainly appreciate it."

Jule lifted her head and caught a glimpse of Dorrie's face peeping from the window. She beckoned, but Dorrie hurriedly moved to the other side of the window.

"I suppose she wants me to bring him a leberwurst sandwich," she told herself, "and he ought not to have it anyway."

Life was very pleasant and simple when viewed from Mr. Wickley's attic room. Things really didn't matter at all up there, and one could dream for hours without interruption. Up in Mr. Wickley's room, for instance, it seemed exceedingly likely that one would become a world-renowned poet. Nowhere else did the scraps of poetry Dorrie carried in her pockets seem as stirring and magnificent as up in the attic bedroom.

In the pocket of her red sweater was a rather melancholy sonnet written with a smudgy lead pencil on a page torn from an old ledger. It was about love, and there were one or two indiscreet allusions to a fair-haired boy with blue eyes. If Linda should find the sonnet—and Linda found everything—she would know instantly that it concerned Phil Lancer. She might even guess that Phil was in love with a girl—Molly Miller—and that Dorrie was foolish enough to resent it.

"Still, she must know that a poem's got to be about one person or another," Dorrie thought, "and probably she'd rather I wrote it about Phil than Steve."

As a matter of fact, Dorrie had written a poem about Steve, too. She was affected by Steve quite intensely. Steve had red hair and smoked a pipe and swore horrible virile oaths. That was fascinating enough in itself; but he was going to run away to sea, someday, and that was the most thrilling thing Dorrie could imagine. He would pack his things in a little bag, some night, and catch the night train to New York and the big boats. She was to know the night it happened and meet him down under the elm tree and say goodbye. She would give him this poem as a farewell present. They would, perhaps, arrange to meet in Madrid or Cairo. Phil Lancer would realize later how important Dorrie Shirley was.

Yesterday she and Phil had gone out to the cider mill and consumed gallons of the delicious liquor. She had remembered to bring back a jugful for Steve because Lew wouldn't let him get off much. Phil had been annoyed in his stolid way.

"You do have the queerest friends, Dorrie," he had said, as if—Dorrie instantly thought—he had heard somebody else, probably Molly Miller, say it first.

"Steve's got ambition, anyway," she defended him. "You wait until he comes home an admiral or something."

"He hasn't gone yet," scoffed Phil. "Sailors aren't so much anyway."

"Better'n farmers," taunted Dorrie. Phil flushed.

"Wait till I get a job in the shoe store," he retorted. "I don't intend to be a hick all my life."

Dorrie was sorry she'd challenged him, then. She began humming and refused, later on, to be drawn into an argument about Molly Miller's beauty. She didn't mind teasing Phil, the stocky halfback with the absurd pompadour, but somehow she couldn't bear to hurt the shy dreamy little boy that he used to be . . .

From the attic window she saw him going home in the dusk from football practice. She called and waved, but Phil did not see her. A man hurrying across from the station, bag in hand, looked up and waved his hat.

"Dick Farley's back," Dorrie informed Mr. Wickley. "He came on the 5:10 from Cincinnati. Marie will cheer up now."

"The all is full of light and invisible darkness," replied the old man, succinctly. "All things are one . . ."

"Do you want some broth now? It's almost supper time," Dorrie suggested, but her host made a gesture of impatience. The room was getting dark, and for the first time he could not read in the dark. He had forgotten that chapter. It frightened him a little. He was getting old. Someday he would die.

Dorrie could see Linda crossing the tracks now.

She was almost running, and even in the half twilight, Dorrie sensed a strange excitement in her sister's bearing.

"Maybe she's seen Courtenay Stall," ejaculated Dorrie.

She looked toward the bed. Her patient had drifted into a doze, the book falling from his gray fingers. She would go down and fix him a bowl of mush and milk. She would be bustling about the kitchen when Linda came in, and her sister would realize that she hadn't stayed home from school for nothing . . . She would wear rubber gloves, too, while she spread his bread . . . and that white cap on the pantry doorknob . . .

* * *

Linda came through the kitchen like a whirlwind. She looked neither to right nor left but rushed to the staircase and flew to her room.

"Now what's got into her?" exclaimed Jule, coming in from the porch. "Have you been aggravating her, Dorrie?"

Dorrie shook her head in a bewildered negative. She dangled one rubber glove from her fingers, disappointed that her nurse business had been so completely ignored. Linda wasn't usually impetuous like that, except when she was in a temper. And when she was in a temper, she always said so.

"Something about the Stalls, I guess," Dorrie said to Jule.

It was.

A glorious thing had happened to Linda Shirley. Courtenay Stall had spoken to her! Not a nod, a distant bow—but actually—heavens, what ecstasy!—"Hello, Linda." "Linda," he had said.

Flung face downward on her bed in an unbearable still delight, Linda went over the whole incident—a few bars of haunting music, a fragment of joy . . . She had just turned the corner to Maple Avenue. She glanced in the millinery window at her reflection. Her little gray hat was perfect, her blue serge as immaculately smooth as the day it was pressed, and her cheeks—she distinctly remembered noting this, and couldn't help feeling that perhaps it helped—were flushed a rich crimson. She was thinking—let me see, what had she been thinking of?—oh, yes, of old Mr. Fitz in the lumber office and how offensively familiar he was getting . . .

Perhaps that was why she was blushing . . .

Well, she had just stepped to the curb, preparing to cross the street, when a roadster slid up—stopped right in front of her, and—good heavens!—it was Courtenay Stall!

She had stepped back, startled. He had looked directly at her, right into her very soul, almost, with his queer mysterious eyes—what did a Stall think about, anyway?—and in a low clear voice he had said:

"Hello, Linda."

—Or no!

It was more intimate, even, than that. It was: "'Lo, Linda."

"Oh-oh," Linda had gasped. "G-good evening."

She hadn't dared say "Courtenay," and she didn't want to say "Mr. Stall." He had gotten out, and she had gone on her way down Maple Avenue, beautiful, gorgeous Maple Avenue. She hadn't dared to look back. What if he had been looking toward her? Her poor heart couldn't have endured such ecstasy.

"'Lo, Linda."

Linda lay on the bed, limp, drenched with a deep, hushed content.

Courtenay Stall had spoken her name.

* * *

Mr. Wickley improved. He began getting letters regularly from Cambridge. Dorrie offered him every opportunity to confide their contents, but he seemed very secretive.

"The poor old man was dying of loneliness," Jule said. "Soon as he got in touch with some of his own kin, he felt all right."

Jule was relieved to have the old man off her mind. There was so many things to trouble her. There was Ella, bursting with nasty stories about Esther Mason, which Jule refused to listen to, and which, therefore, Ella yearned to drop in Linda's indignant ear; as if Linda wasn't difficult enough to keep in leash, without hearing tales about the unfortunate little bride.

Every time Esther came into Jule's kitchen for a friendly chat, the old woman was on pins and needles lest her older grandchild walk in and order the caller out.

"I've never known her to feel so strong about any of the lodgers," reflected Jule. "She can't hear Esther's name without going into fits. It's a good thing the Winslows have gone, too, or she'd be sure to say something to poor little Mrs. Winslow."

There was that matter of the Winslows, too. It still puzzled Jule.

No one knew how it happened. One morning Mr. Winslow's magazine came in the same mail with Mrs. Winslow's. Dorrie had given the lady hers, and, after she had climbed breathlessly up to her room to peruse it, the faithful Dorrie had run over to the drugstore to give Mr. Winslow his.

The ex-actor was all alone in the store, leaning in a posture of melancholy grace on the toothbrush counter. His eye brightened at the sight of Dorrie. He hurriedly tore open the wrapper and began to scan the columns with a voracious zest which Dorrie found quite mystifying.

"Maybe his name's in it," she concluded, identifying his excitement with Ella's, when perusing the *Birchfield News* for some such item as: "Mrs. Ralph Purkiss of Marion passed Wednesday last with her second cousin, Miss Ella Morris of 14 Elm Street."

"Ah-h-h!" suddenly exclaimed Mr. Winslow, fastening a paragraph with the aesthetic nail of his index finger. "The old company's reorganized, and playing—by Jove!—in Mansfield this week. When's November 30? Why—that's today!"

His face began to glow. Dorrie was willing to discuss the matter until the thought should occur to him that inasmuch as the owner was not around, there was no reason why he should not invite her to a soda. He usually did.

Today he seemed quite oblivious to Dorrie after his first excited exclamation. She sat on a fountain stool in a casual easy way, waiting for him to finish the magazine.

"Mr. Winslow, have you picked out a house yet?" she asked, pleasantly. "I saw Mrs. Winslow hemming towels and doilies last night."

"A house, a house?" vaguely repeated the actor, looking at Dorrie with a far-off expression. "Oh, of course—yes, Mrs. Winslow is making plans for everything, right along."

For some reason his face grew suddenly sad. He drummed the counter with his fingers. He absently turned a yellow cardboard Coca-Cola lady upside down. Down the street a red streetcar, the hourly car from Mansfield to Galion, lumbered across Maple Avenue. Mr. Winslow grew gay again. He beamed at Dorrie. He swaggered up to the soda fountain.

"What will it be, my child?" he boomed, in a vibrant fortissimo which the drugstore acoustics did not require. "Vanilla or chocolate?"

Dorrie ordered chocolate with a sigh of relief. She studied Mr. Winslow through the mirror as she ate her sundae. He was standing in the back corner—of course he'd forgotten she could see him in the mirror—going through a most elaborate series of gestures . . .

"Did you ever think of going on the stage?" he politely asked her, after a moment. "A wonderful profession, my dear. A beautiful life . . ."

"Oh, yes," Dorrie said in a matter-of-fact way. "I expect I'll be an actress someday, maybe. In New York City."

"Really," Mr. Winslow approved. "That makes me very happy, my dear child. I welcome you gladly to our glorious ranks."

"I thought you didn't like it," Dorrie put in.

Mr. Winslow shrugged his shoulders.

"That shows what a real actor I am if you received that impression. Acting is—well, no one will ever know to what heights I might have aspired. But the wife isn't strong enough, you know. Too hard for a delicately bred lady. Yes . . ." and he paused in wiping up the marble counter to gaze out the window thoughtfully, "Mrs. Winslow is just a little homebody, you know, a real treasure."

Dorrie went on to school thoughtfully. That afternoon she found her grandmother in a state of worried perplexity.

"Mrs. Winslow's gone," Jule announced abruptly. "She packed up this morning, paid me right up to the minute, and took the two o'clock car to Mansfield. She left a note for the mister on her dresser. I can't understand it. They were as loving as two turtledoves. Always thinking of each other."

"What did the note say?" Dorrie inquired.

"It was sealed," returned Jule. "But as near as I could make out through the light it was something about a clipper. I declare, it's very funny."

"Wait till we see what he says," Dorrie suggested.

But Mr. Winslow did not come back. At night a boy came over from the drugstore with a magazine which Mr. Winslow had wished his wife to see. He was leaving Birchfield and the magazine would explain, the boy reported.

"Where did he go?" asked Jule anxiously.

"To Mansfield," said the boy.

Jule and Dorrie exchanged a mystified glance. Jule tapped the arm of her chair nervously for a moment.

"Now what do you suppose?" Jule murmured. "They were going to build such a lovely little home. Why they took an option on the Burgess place . . . We won't say anything to Linda about the queer way they went off. I wish I understood stage people. I'm bound to admit it's almost like Linda says. There's always that funny streak in 'em."

* * *

Mrs. Lew Mason was as happy as a lark. From morning to midnight she sang about her work and flung cheerful banalities to Aunt Jule. In her dark little kitchen she bloomed like a great poppy, her black eyes flashing with a new luster and her cheeks a brilliant scarlet. When Jule was puttering about the kitchen making piccalilli or sauerkraut, she often smiled gently at Esther's shrill soprano soaring joyously through "Silver Threads among the Gold" and "Oh, You Beautiful Lady."

"Little bride's happy," Jule commented sometimes to Ella Morris.

"Humph!" was invariably Ella's reply.

Ella had a devastating curiosity about Esther and sometimes chatted with her chiefly for the purpose of satisfying that curiosity. She really felt embarrassed, as she told Aunt Jule, when Mayor Riggs or Mrs. Remer gossiped about Esther Mason, and here she was, right in the same house with the girl and not a word to say, for or against. Why, it was humiliating indeed to have things going on under your very nose and you not knowing a thing!

Jule automatically sympathized with Ella, and the next moment was consoling Esther for what Esther termed Ella's "nosiness."

Esther was a very good-natured soul. She frequently offered help to Aunt Jule in making the beds and never failed to do whatever Jule might ask. About the only favor Jule ever requested was that she play the piano. Linda, who had learned to play the piano at Mary Jane's house, refused to touch her grandmother's unique instrument. But Esther never refused. She sat down and pounded through a selection with all the zest she had been wont to put into the farmhouse parlor organ. Jule would rock gently to the music, her eyes closed, unmindful of the fact that she had actually heard but half a dozen notes.

"Now that's real nice," she would say gratefully. "What was the name of that piece, Esther?"

"'Angel's Serenade,'" Esther would reply, and then, with a wink at Dorrie, "It certainly is a swell piano, Aunt Jule."

But when Linda was home, Esther kept discreetly to her own quarters. Jule felt sorry for her in a way, though there was something impish rather than pathetic in Esther's reaction to Linda. Instead of being crushed by Linda's not infrequent insults, she often looked as if she were ready to burst out laughing. Her humility was too stressed, her modest withdrawings too pronounced for sincerity. Linda felt this at least, and it increased her passionate dislike of the girl.

If Esther was in Jule's kitchen, Linda went up to her room and came out in the upper hallway sometime later to call down in a cold voice: "Dorrie, has that woman gone yet?"

Sometimes Esther would hear this insulting query and would wink broadly at Marie or Jule or burst into outright laughter.

"Aunt Jule," Ella Morris hissed, after one of these episodes, "do you realize that Lew Mason's wife is making fun of Linda Shirley? Why, did you hear that laugh? Yes, sir, she's making a fool of Linda!"

"Oh no, Ella," Jule protested, her broad forehead contracted for an instant. "Esther doesn't mean any harm. She thinks the world of Linda."

"Yes?" significantly retorted the invalid. "You don't know some of the things I know about that woman. Why! . . ."

She made a clucking noise, fraught with insinuations.

"Ella," Jule said reproachfully, "you don't mean to be, but you're two-faced. You were nice to that little lady when she was here a minute ago. And the minute she's gone you say things about her. I don't like that in you, Ella. If you don't like Esther you oughtn't to pretend you do. It's not right."

"Who said I didn't like her?" exclaimed Ella in great astonishment. "Why I'm as fond of her as you are. I don't say she's a good girl 'cause I happen to know she ain't, but as for liking her—why, Jule, now that she's come, I don't know what the place ever did without her."

Her tone was more than convincing. She tatted silently for a while, though her lips moved noiselessly. She was mentally reframing the conversation for Mrs. Miller's ears, when that great lady should call tomorrow.

"What is it they all tell you about Esther?" Dorrie demanded curiously.

"Tut!" sharply rebuked Jule.

Ella smiled a faint, knowing smile. She held up an inch of lace critically for a moment and then graciously asked Dorrie to wheel her chair a little closer to the gaslight above the table. She had no intention of making any revelations to Dorrie. Dorrie was about as unsatisfactory an audience as her grandmother. She never comprehended asterisks, for instance, and without asterisks there is no gossip. Mrs. Johnnie Ruggles takes the ten o'clock train to Cleveland. Mr. Red Turner takes the afternoon train. Between these two periodic sentences Ella constructed a choice row of potent asterisks.

Yet, when such items were significantly told to Jule or to Dorrie, those two stupids couldn't see a thing in it. As for Linda, she cried about things like that.

"Oh, Ella, what will people say?" she would sob. "They know Red Turner is our nearest neighbor . . . No wonder Mrs. Remer stared right through me this morning."

So Ella allowed her nice little mound of tidbits about Esther to wait for Birchfield's more aristocratic and appreciative ears. On Jule Shirley and her two girls it was absolutely wasted.

Ella enjoyed life thoroughly. Yet people always referred to her as "poor Ella Morris." Poor Ella was quite young, not much over thirty, and it was a frightful thing to go through life a hopeless cripple. Few people sensed the truth about Ella—that the trainwreck which made her a life invalid eight years before had changed her from an ugly, sour potential spinster into—at least in her own eyes—the popular mistress of a salon. Never had a man spoken to Ella Morris until that trainwreck. Never had the Birchfield elite paid more than passing tribute to old Senator Morris's orphaned niece. But with Ella a life invalid, the town, under the leadership of Mrs. Remer and Mrs. Stall, set out to do its duty by her. Ella bloomed and accepted gifts with queenly graciousness.

The good people of the town collected $100 each Christmas to give to Ella. It was considered a duty to call on poor Ella once a week and exchange harmless gossip with her, that she might not feel out of touch with the world. The Elks sent her a yearly gift of $50. The country club sent her books and candy. And in these attentions Ella blushingly read a tribute to her female magnetism.

"I was out in the yard when Carrie Meredith went past today," she would say, with an indulgent smirk to Jule. "She went right by without speaking. Well, thinks I, what's the matter with Carrie Meredith? And what do you suppose it was?"

"She didn't see you," Jule would offer absently.

"See me? Of course she saw me. She's jealous, that's all, because her beau came to see me last night. She's supposed to be engaged to Charley Tait, you know . . . Well! He came in last night with a magazine—the *Designer*—and I don't know what got into the man. He stayed until nearly two o'clock. But my goodness, we were just talking! Even if Charley had—er—said anything or tried anything out of the way, I would have put him in his place quick enough! And how can I help it if he pays attention to me? . . . Honestly, the way I feel is that if a girl can't hold her beau, she can't blame another girl for attracting him!"

With which Ella would hum softly to herself for a little while. If the *Designer* had a love story in it she would toss it with a scornful laugh on the table.

"Isn't that just like a man? I don't see why they always bring me love stories. Just look at that illustration there, will you? That's the kind of mushy stuff they bring me to read. I'm sure I don't know what's in their minds."

She was really much concerned when Mrs. Stall didn't come to see her for two weeks. Of course she knew at once why it was. Her husband had been coming in two or three evenings a week to see Ella, and you couldn't expect a wife to stand for that long.

"Though I don't see why she blames me," Ella confided to Jule. "Goodness knows I wouldn't make trouble between them for worlds. Why, I only think of Will Stall as a good friend . . . And he's always acted like a perfect gentleman. Naturally I saw to that."

When Mrs. Stall appeared next day with some excuse about having had rheumatism, Ella preserved her original opinion. It was a pleasant conceit and harmed no one. She herself did not mention her caller's negligence but chatted affably about other affairs. After all, you couldn't twit a man's wife with being jealous of you. You had to reassure her—make her feel that no matter how insistent her husband might be (and all husbands, to Ella, were libertines in leash), you would never permit him to be unfaithful to his wife. And Ella tactfully withdrew to other topics.

"Why, I says, Mrs. Shirley, how can you say I don't like the girl? Well, she says, you act so cold when she's around. Naturally, I says, you can't expect me to make friends with her. My friends wouldn't allow me to, and what would my uncle, the senator, say if he knew I was being intimate with Lew Mason's wife? . . . But it makes it very hard for me, Mrs. Stall really—very hard."

* * *

Jule had made evasive promises to Linda, after the Winslows left, that she would take no more stage people.

"I wish you'd take schoolteachers and people like that," Linda suggested, "since you must take roomers. Nice people like Mrs. White takes."

Jule gave an audible snort of disgust.

"I'd do washings before I'd take people like that for a living," she ejaculated. "Schoolteachers! Might as well be dead. I like a little life around the place."

Linda bit her lip.

It was, fortunately, after she had left for the office that the Seven Janes arrived at Jule's. Dorrie saw them in Red Turner's shack as she started out to school and promptly abandoned school thoughts to rush back home. She ran across the snowy lawn and pell-mell into the kitchen, her small oval face rosy with excitement.

"There's a lot of actresses at Red Turner's!" she cried. "I know they're actresses because they've all got plumes on their hats, and one of 'em's got a big white fur. And they're coming here too because Red was pointing this way. There's a lot of baggage on the station platform, all marked up with Chicago and New York. Do you suppose they're the Seven Janes that are going to play at the Star this week?"

"They can't play at the Star," Ella Morris put in. She was benignly helping Jule hem up some dish towels. "The platform caved in last week with that strongwoman and her elephant. Mayor Riggs was saying last night that he guessed he'd have to put in a few new boards before the new company came, only he was so busy, what with two men in jail at once, all this week that he didn't see how he was going to get around to it. Guess he'll have to sell that theater."

"Wouldn't it be wonderful if they all stayed here?" Dorrie glowed. "I've never seen so many actresses all at once. I'd better stay home today and help fix up cots in Miss Bellow's room, in case they do come."

Jule did not protest. She smoothed her handsome black hair a bit, adjusted the lace collar on her housedress, and bade Dorrie brighten up the piano with a vase of paper poinsettias, now obscured by the goldfish bowl.

The Seven Janes came over about ten o'clock, accompanied by their manager, to engage a room to rest in while they waited for "Lima to wire."

"We can't play the Star," explained the man, "so I'm telegraphing to Lima and Youngstown to see if we can get billed there for this week."

Jule welcomed them joyously, without even recalling the half-promise she had given Linda. Dorrie stood modestly in the background, thrilling to the marrow over her propinquity to real actresses. She couldn't have been more impressed if they had all been Bernhardts . . .

They were a shabby, hardworking little group of troupers, all fairly young, and not at all the painted, flamboyant hussies the bill-posters had advertised. Dorrie was a little disappointed. Still, an actress was an actress . . . How wonderful if she could join a company someday when it came to her grandmother's and go to strange exotic places like South Bend, Dayton, or even Louisville. To wear glittering slithering dresses and satin slippers . . . and a bandeau of brilliants in her hair . . . How proud Linda would be of her . . . But, on second thought, probably Linda would not be so proud as she ought to be.

She was fascinated by the girls and hung about staring at them so that her services were of no value to Jule. When the girls collected in the absent music teacher's room, Dorrie followed them shyly and watched them in a sort of trance.

There was a little one with sleek black hair and a green velvet dress, who was called "Peaches." She was very quiet. She sat at the window, looking out and taking no part in the others' conversation. The manager had gone to the station to do his telegraphing. Dorrie saw him squeeze Peaches's hand as he went out.

"Manager's pet!" hissed the big dark girl they called Marg. "How does it feel to be in love with a married man, Peaches old thing?"

"Yes?" murmured Peaches, unruffled.

"Don't disturb her. She's gotta watch him out the window to see that he doesn't pick up any village blonde," sneered the one with the strange red hair. "You can't be sure of that guy, can you, Peaches?"

Peaches's thin red lip curled a little, but she said nothing. Chin in hand, she kept her eyes fixed out the window.

"Wonder who it'll be in Lima?" pursued Marg. "Remember, it was Dot in Bucyrus and Tess in Galion. Might be Molly or Vi in Lima. Bobby believes in giving everybody their chance."

Peaches smiled a secret little smile and pointedly twisted an enormous diamond ring on her finger.

"She's wearing that stage diamond he gave her to show us he's going to marry her the minute he gets a divorce," mocked the red-haired one. "Oh, dearie, ain't you the trusting little ingenue, though?"

"Must be nice being the manager's little friend," piped up a skinny little thing with great blue eyes. "Taking encores when nobody claps. Getting bouquets on Saturday nights and suppers in his room. Pretty soft, eh, Peaches?"

Peaches flushed a little then but maintained her scornful silence. When the man appeared in the doorway—(without even knocking, and the girls were in their petticoats)—Peaches lifted her delicately penciled eyebrows significantly and arose.

"No luck yet, girls," he said, affably. He was a big bland man with a slight yellow mustache, half concealing the loose wide mouth. On the stage he was very handsome.

"Supposing we take a walk," suggested Peaches, taking his arm with a possessive air, which she knew was galling to her envious companions.

"Sure. See the town," agreed the man. He pinched her affectionately on the thigh, and Peaches blushed in delicate pleasure.

"Common lot," Marg said to Dorrie, as the two went out. "It's girls like that that gives the stage such a bad name. Why, I'd no more think of such goings-on!"

The little skinny one sat down at the piano on which Miss Bellows's tearful pupils struggled through "Rustic Dance" and "Narcissus." She began to play a syncopated air, crashing out every third note and bouncing rhythmically up and down on the seat. She chanted the words in a thin, shrill voice:

> Come, Josephine, in my flying machine,
> Going up she goes, up she goes.
> Balance yourself like a bird on the beam,
> In the air she goes, there she goes.
> Up, up a little bit higher!
> Oh, oh, the moon is on fire!
> Come Josephine, in my flying machine,
> Going up—all on—goodbye!

"Shut up, Tess!" pleaded the plump rosy little one they called Molly. "Every time you bounce I lose a stitch."

She was sitting in the corner, sewing on some vivid green satin, and Dorrie wondered why she hadn't teased Peaches the way the others had.

"Say, kiddie." She beckoned Dorrie. "Has your grandmother got a sewing machine?"

Dorrie led her up to the attic where the sewing machine was kept. She stayed to explain the bobbin and also to bask in contact with this great actress. Only she wished the actress would talk about the stage and act really dramatic instead of being so absorbed in making a nightgown out of sea green satin, with spangled shoulder straps.

"It's much too pretty for a nightgown," Dorrie told her earnestly.

Molly studied a cluster of rosebuds absently.

"Oh, I don't know," she murmured. "A nightgown is, after all, a nightgown . . . Say, Lima's quite a place, isn't it?"

Dorrie didn't know what Lima had to do with it. She wished she had a green satin nightgown with gold spangles and little strings of rosebuds.

"It's so beautiful," she sighed again, lovingly fingering the texture.

"I'd hate to tell you how many meals that cost me," confessed Molly. "And I didn't lose but eight pounds."

Peaches and Forster wandered up and down Main Street all day. Dorrie saw them having a soda in the drugstore when she went out for groceries. She saw them on the river bridge late in the afternoon. Forster had his arm flung over Peaches and was laughing in an indolent teasing way. Peaches's face was flushed and happy.

At Aunt Jule's the girls talked venomously of the "manager's pet"— that is, all except Molly. Molly sewed on her green satin nightgown, her lips closed in a thin absorbed line and a faraway look in her eyes.

"And the way she grabs his arm!" Marg exclaimed disgustedly, watching the pair coming up the front walk. "You'd think the girl owned Bobby Forster."

"The point is," Molly said, threading her needle, "she doesn't."

It was a thrilling day for Dorrie. She was sorry when the big fair man came back with tickets for the five o'clock train. She had hoped they would stay several days, and perhaps—oh, she daren't think them and be an actress, too!

Peaches went into the kitchen and asked for a basin of hot water to wash out a poor shred of a pink silk camisole. She put it on again, still wet.

Jule was scandalized and offered to lend her the big muslin boned kind she wore.

"Oh, no," Peaches smiled gently. "I have another, but I like this one. It has more style."

"Nobody's going to see it," urged Aunt Jule. "And you mark my words, you'll catch pleurisy in that damp thing."

Peaches shook her sleek black head.

"You know, I wish we were going to stay here," she murmured presently. "I don't think I'll like Lima as well."

"Molly's glad you're going there," Dorrie said. "She says she bets she'll have a good time when you get to Lima."

Peaches's eyes narrowed a little—became widely frightened a little later on intercepting a meditative, appraising glance Forster gave to Molly's figure . . .

Dorrie watched them wistfully as they started off to the station, Peaches now content, arm in arm with the big man, bland, expressionless, loose-lipped . . . The girls followed in shrill, giggling little groups. All except Molly, who loitered, a little abstracted, behind the others. She waved to Dorrie from the other side of the track.

"Gee, I wish I could be an actress," sighed Dorrie, reluctantly coming into the house.

"Maybe you will," indulgently answered her grandmother from the kitchen. "But right now you'd better take a knife and scrape off the gum they left all over the furniture."

Linda came hurrying up the back stairs with quick light steps.

"Grandma! Did you let those actresses stay after you told me—"

Dorrie heard Jule's calm answer after a moment. "I declare it's something awful the chops that new butcher sends. They're nothing but bone."

Chapter Three

D orrie would be sixteen in May.
She looked anxiously in Linda's mirror for signs of growing maturity, but to her disappointed eyes, her face was exactly the same rounded, childish affair it had been since she was six.

She probably wouldn't grow a bit taller, she thought pessimistically, and Linda would always be a head higher. She had often imagined the comradely chats she and Linda would have when she became sixteen. By that time she would be a suave, sophisticated woman of the world who went to Lutheran Bible class parties and sometimes had a beau bring her home. When people would tease her about her suitors, she would get very angry and leave the room.

She would go to Max's Saturday night dances, too. Linda could have her country club, but the joyous sounds issuing from the Elks' Hall on Saturday nights were far more stimulating to Dorrie than the refined laughter of the every second Wednesday dances of the club.

Yet here was sixteen not two weeks off, and Dorrie found herself not the least bit grown up—slight, with that absurd infantile tilt to her nose! Perhaps when she was eighteen . . . Linda was eighteen now, and in all probability that was the age of vital changes.

Jule was making Dorrie a new dress for her birthday. It was white embroidery over pink satin—Mrs. Winslow's pink satin. Dorrie was certain there wouldn't be any prettier dress than hers at the commencement exercises this year.

"Don't get married until you're twenty, Dorrie," Marie Farley earnestly advised her on the morning of her birthday, when Dorrie came in to display her new gown.

"Oh, I don't know," Dorrie replied, intimating dozens of chances. "A girl marry, really . . . Just look at Linda. I hate to have Linda an old maid."

"But wait two years at least," Marie urged. "Eighteen will be time enough. You won't know your own mind, you see, till then."

"Well—I don't know," reluctantly replied Dorrie, toying with her handkerchief. "You see there's two."

"Already? Not really?" Marie's tone was astonished and flattering.

"One is a boy—er—man I've known for years," improvised Dorrie. "I like him, but in a platonic way. Maybe it wouldn't be fair for me to marry him."

Marie was inclined to agree with this.

"The other," breathed Dorrie, "is an officer in the navy. Terribly handsome. He is so—so intense, too."

"An officer?" asked Marie, quite impressed. "An ensign, perhaps."

"A colonel," Dorrie said.

Marie reflected on this for a moment.

"Dorrie" she said, presently, "if you want my frank opinion, I wouldn't advise you to marry either of those men."

"I think you're right, Marie," Dorrie agreed in some relief. "It wouldn't be wise."

She left Marie as hastily as she could. The discussion had been carried, she felt, a little beyond the point of discretion. But back in Linda's room, she looked in the mirror with awed, gratified eyes.

"You *are* grown up," she told her reflection, respectfully.

Old enough, actually old enough to be advised against marriage!

* * *

It was very queer about Phil Lancer. Dorrie couldn't quite puzzle the thing out. He never stopped for her anymore on his way to school. He sometimes didn't see her when she came into the classroom. Whenever Dorrie talked to him, he seemed preoccupied and embarrassed.

"I guess he's going around with Molly Miller's crowd," thought Dorrie. "He doesn't want me to feel badly about being left out, so he doesn't tell me things anymore."

He needn't bother about her feelings, though. *She* didn't care for parties, anyway. She didn't want any intimate friends. She had too many delightful things to think about. She never stayed after school to gossip with the girls (nor did they encourage her) but hurried home as fast as her legs would carry her. You never could tell what fascinating strangers might have gotten off the afternoon train and be sitting at that very moment in Jule's parlor . . . Jule's place, in fact, was far too absorbing for Dorrie to waste much thought on Birchfield school affairs.

"Who's taking you to the commencement exercises?" Linda asked Dorrie one morning. Linda wasn't going to her office that day. She had a headache. She stood in the front doorway while her younger sister dallied on the steps until the last possible moment for starting to school.

"I don't know," answered Dorrie, idly swinging her book bag. "Maybe I won't go, if I don't have to. I'm not in the glee club, you see."

"Isn't Phil Lancer going?" Linda asked, curiously.

Dorrie flushed a little.

"He's taking Molly Miller," she replied, casually. "We don't see much of each other anymore."

A bleak pallor swept over Linda's face. The blight of Jule Shirley's place had at last touched Dorrie! Linda looked at Dorrie with a strange new compassion.

"I haven't had a chance to talk to Phil for ages," Dorrie said with a little perplexed frown. "I called to him the other day, but I guess he didn't hear me. Probably thinking about Molly."

Linda gripped the doorknob. She knew why Phil's attitude toward Jule Shirley's granddaughter had changed. And it wasn't Molly Miller, either. He was growing up and beginning to understand things. He was realizing what Jule's place signified.

At that moment Dorrie caught sight of Phil's stocky figure coming up the road. She waved and called to him.

"Hello, Phil! Wait till I get my sweater, will you?"

The boy, his hands in his pockets, and his eyes bent on the road ahead, did not hear. Dorrie called louder . . . He was only a few yards away, but he didn't look up. Dorrie's jaw dropped. Puzzled and hurt, she looked after him as he hurried past. Presently she turned around and saw that Linda had been watching from the doorway. And from Linda's face she suddenly knew . . .

"Oh, Linda," she whispered, incredulously. "He heard me."

She sat down on the stone steps and put her head in her hands. She felt Linda's fingers on her shoulder.

"You see? You're beginning to understand, now," Linda said in a low, bitter tone. "We live in 'Jule's Place.' Nice people don't know us. Don't cry. Life will always be like that. Unless someday we get out of this cursed house. Oh, Dorrie—" Linda's voice quivered a little, "living in 'Jule's place' has ruined both our lives. She's to blame for everything."

Dorrie lifted her head.

"'Tisn't Grandma," she denied, passionately. "It's Phil who's spoiled everything!"

She put her arm before her eyes—eyes blurred with the memory of a blonde boy and slim, little girl running through a golden wheat field singing school songs.

Dorrie Shirley was slowly becoming a woman.

* * *

Sometimes Linda sat by the window in her room, watching dusk envelop the tall white birches that fringed the railroad track. Tragic-eyed, her chin cupped in her hands, she would review her misery.

Outcast.

She belonged to "Aunt Jule's Place." Decent people didn't even know her first name. Birchfield thought she must be bad like Esther Mason. Cheap like the tenth-rate actresses who stopped there. Dirty like Lew. Queer like Mr. Wickley . . . One of Jule's folks. Trash.

To Birchfield, she was one of those people who lived in the big, black house beyond the railroad, who stared gawkily at all the good people of Birchfield flying by in their Fords, who gaped when one called on poor Ella Morris. Fast women stopped at that black house, and common people from the trains . . . One scarcely dared speak to the proprietress of such an establishment or to the two waifs under her care.

"I know how they feel," Linda thought. "I would feel that way, too, if I were in their place."

She stared somberly across the white trees.

Beyond those white birches lay the smug little white homes of Maple Avenue, Walnut Street, and Main Street . . . Respectability . . . Beauty.

They were one and the same to Linda as they were to Birchfield. She belonged over there with those untainted people . . . Linda shook herself. Dreams like this were fantastic. For her there would never be anything but the sordid monotony of Jule's. Years stretched before her wide, despairing eyes . . . years of gray misery.

And now the blight had touched Dorrie, too.

Linda wondered how Dorrie would take it. Would she, too, suddenly loathe the place and all its people for stamping her in the eyes of the world? Dorrie, after all, had no Courtenay Stall to pray for, to lift her eventually from this mire. The Lancer boy was a mere farmer.

Linda was puzzled by the manner in which Dorrie actually did accept Phil's snub. Instead of showing a new disgust with her surroundings after her boy chum had indicated how damaging they were to her social eligibility, she professed a profound disgust with Phil. She appalled even Ella by declaring that Lew Mason was a lot nicer than Phil—that Esther was a lot prettier than Molly Miller, and that Gertrude Stall was a fat goop. And another time she said that when she got rich, she was going to build a house exactly like her grandmother's—smoke-colored and square, only a little nearer to the railroad track so that she could wave to the passengers . . . Linda did not see how her own sister could be so crassly lacking in ideals.

No, Dorrie did not propose to worry herself over Phil Lancer. Why should she waste time on a farm boy when a real baron occupied a room in her own house? A short, dumpy little baron, it is true, but you could forget his appearance by just concentrating on his alluring name—"Baron George Friedrich August von Sturm."

Oh, it was a marvelous thing to have a real nobleman under your roof. Think of his having selected Birchfield, of all places, as the spot from which he was to study America! It was miraculous.

Of course, the good people of Birchfield, when informed through the Ella Morris News Service, laughed heartily at the idea of a real baron staying at Aunt Jule's. It was, in their opinion, most absurd. Why should a baron come to Birchfield, and why should he pick out Aunt Jule's when he could go to a good hotel in Cleveland or Mansfield and really see some sights? Yes, Birchfield placed small stock in the authenticity of Dorrie's baron.

He was a small, pale man with watery blue eyes and a stiff yellow mustache. He walked all about town, carrying a stout Malacca stick and wearing a funny little round tweed hat.

Birchfield people were always seeing him walking briskly along some country road. Sometimes they called from the genial luxury of their Ford autos, "Want a ride?" and were bewildered and disgusted when the man pretended he'd rather walk. The baron was looney, was Birchfield's verdict at length.

"Beautiful country," he would glow to some dumbfounded farmer as he swung along the road. "Beautiful."

"Poor for corn, this here stretch," the farmer would answer, looking at the man with ill-concealed suspicion. Beautiful! A fine thing to say about one's crops.

Linda caught the town attitude toward the baron and treated him with contemptuous aloofness. If he was a real baron, he was a foreigner, and therefore worthy of disgust; if he was a fake baron, then he was equally worthy of contempt. Jule referred to him as a nice little fellow, as quiet and refined as any roomer she'd ever had. He had a shelf full of German books in blinding print, and Dorrie, who had passed remotely through two years of German, saw a fine opportunity to make an impression.

"I've read *Glück Auf,*" she said, eagerly. Yes, that was the name of the brown book one took to German class. "I—I liked it so much."

The baron was politely impressed. He was amused at Dorrie, but he could not take his eyes away from Linda's fair beauty.

"My, wouldn't you like to be a baroness?" snickered Ella to Linda. "Maybe you could if you played your cards right. Go to foreign countries and travel and such. My!"

"I don't like foreigners," replied Linda. "And I don't like foreign countries. What if he is a baron? He's only a foreigner. Why, he can't even speak good English!"

But baron or no baron, he was at least a gentleman, and Linda relented a little after a few days, sufficiently to bid him good morning or exchange an occasional remark. Decent people were rare enough in Jule's rooms . . . He called the girls Fräulein Linda and Fräulein Dorrie. And frequently he bowed over old Jule's hand with a ravishing courtliness. Dorrie was thrilled and tried not to see his pale, watery eyes.

"A baron," she whispered to herself. "A real baron."

Sometimes she caught him staring at Linda with a wistful interest. She was so sorry for him, for of course he must have fallen in love with Linda. One night she saw him going into Miss Bellows's room where Linda was dusting, his arms full of Kodak albums. Dorrie had seen them—pictures of a funny old castle on top of a hill, and pictures of the baron on a white horse, and pictures of the baron and another man in breeches walking through a marshy field with some dogs and guns. There were pictures of queer cities, too, and quaint little villages.

"Fräulein Linda, please—" he stammered. "These are the pictures I wanted to show you. There are some of Munich. You would like Munich, Fräulein."

Linda wiped the keys of the piano.

"Just leave them," she said, indifferently, without glancing up. "If I have time, I'll look at them. Ella will probably want to see them, anyway."

The baron, flushing a little, laid the albums on the round, walnut table.

"You are very beautiful, Fräulein," he blurted out. "I have admired you so much... Your hair..."

His hands twitched as if he should like to touch it. Linda looked up in faint annoyance.

"If you would let me talk to you, Fräulein—" he hurried on, catching her frown.

"Really, I am very busy," she interrupted coldly. The baron's face fell. He came over to her side.

"I have known you so short a time, but never—never have I seen anyone so beautiful," he sighed. "It is much to ask, when you know me so little, but—"

"I must go," Linda said abruptly.

The baron looked at her sorrowfully, and then his eye lit up with an eager hope. He put out a hand to detain her.

"At least, Fräulein Linda, you will let me sing for you? That is so little to ask."

Without waiting for her reply, he sat down at the piano, a short, saggy little man with a dropping blonde mustache and very tight trousers. His blue eyes were fixed with rapt intensity on Linda. She shrugged, and stood still.

Du bist wie eine Blume,
So hod und schön und rein
Ich schau dich an und Wehmut
Schleicht mir, ins Herz hinein—

His voice was husky and a little choked. Linda's eyes were chilly and disgusted. She made no attempt to conceal her boredom.

"Fräulein does not like love songs?" asked the baron, his eyes on her face.

"Oh, yes, but—"

"Perhaps it is my voice?"

"No, I—"

"I think I understand," said the little man, steadily. "It is both. Fräulein does not like *my* singing of love songs."

Linda's poise was a little shaken by the odd, steady gaze of the baron. She picked up her dustcloth and started for the door.

"Perhaps that was it," she said, a little self-consciously. She'd never heard of such a thing! A man wanting to sing for you as if it meant something! "Good night, Baron."

She hurried down the hall and failed to notice the figure of Dorrie huddled outside the door until she heard her accusing whisper.

"Oh, Linda, you're just hateful! If a baron made love to *me,* I'll bet I'd know what to do."

So moved was Dorrie by Linda's cruel chilling of the baron's flame that she slid down to the floor again and cried. When the baron came out she was going to be very kind to him.

But the baron sat for a long time at the piano, one stubby white hand silently holding the last chord of the song. His lips, without making a sound, formed words, "*Du bist wie eine Blume.*"

* * *

The very day the baron went away, Marie and Dick Farley moved to their new home way up by the boulevard. Dick was working in the factory now, and Marie was much happier, though she told Aunt Jule she would miss the "dear, funny old place."

Linda and Dorrie went to call on her in the little house way up near the new boulevard soon after she was settled. She seemed more and more absorbed in her coming baby and said very little about New York, beyond expressing the wish that she and Dick had saved all the money for furniture that they had flung on taxis and theaters during their courtship.

She had ceased to bother about her looks in the house. After all, who was going to see her if she did brush her hair back in that new French way, or penciled her eyebrows into a delicate arch, or wore a dress with that new pleated insert? Marie lolled on the wicker couch in a somewhat rumpled kimono, and her hair looked like any other Birchfield woman's hair.

Coming home from their call, Linda was silent. She read an arrogant happiness into Marie's careless acceptance of domesticity. Marie must have reached that enviable stage where things like hair and neatness didn't matter, she was so assured of her satisfactory future. Linda resented it.

"Goodness, it must be dull living all alone in a house," Dorrie exclaimed, feelingly. "Poor Marie! If I get married I'm going to have a lot of boarders around so there'll be things going on all the time."

"Don't be stupid and common," Linda retorted.

"But, Linda," protested Dorrie, skipping to keep up with Linda's swift stride, "there's never anything new happening when you're all alone in a little house like that. At Grandma's you never know who the trains are going to bring in, and you never know what's going to happen next."

"No," said Linda, sardonically. "You're right."

"I imagine Marie misses our house a lot," Dorrie ended, confidently. "Don't you?"

Miss Jule's house? Miss those vulgar people? Linda's mouth twisted into an ironic smile. Dorrie was a funny girl. You would think she was old enough to have all of those queer notions out of her head.

"Everybody thinks *we're* missing a lot being stuck away in that old prison," Linda said, nodding toward the house. "I know I shall never be happy until I live in a house of my own just like Marie's."

She bit her lip, then, and became very brusque. She was always sorry after she had betrayed anything of herself in her conversation. Dorrie, for her part, was always grateful for these sisterly confidences. She tried to want a little house too so that she might flatter Linda by agreeing with her. But it really wasn't any use trying. The very thought weighed on her.

"Here comes Courtenay Stall," Dorrie announced, as a red roadster loomed up over the hill.

She felt Linda's hand on her arm tighten, but Linda preserved an impassive face as the car approached. It slid past them, and Dorrie could not be sure, but it looked almost as if Courtenay had nodded. She looked at Linda. The latter's face was dyed a deep rose, and her blue eyes seemed suddenly to blaze with an inner excitement. He *had* nodded. If his car had not been going so fast, perhaps he might have spoken.

"My wish is coming true," Linda thought and then closed her eyes for an instant. Oh, the thing *had* to happen! It *had* to happen!

Dorrie, after a thoughtful glance upward at her sister, found herself wondering how Linda could get so excited over an insignificant person like Courtenay Stall. Why, he was really plain, with his mother's fishy blue eyes, and his receding chin, and his father's bristly hair. He was big-boned like his mother but not heavy. Usually, his big, loose body gave an air of lazy, brutal power. He walked always with his shoulders humped and his hands in his pockets. Dorrie couldn't see a thing princely in Courtenay Stall's exterior. He wore loud red and black sweaters and funny little caps.

He had worn things like that all through college and apparently expected to make it his permanent style. If it weren't for these promiscuous symbols he would have been a most uninteresting looking person. Yet in the very insignificance of his features, Linda saw the discreet aristocrat. Actual beauty would have been too garish, Linda felt, for him. Aristocracy was too perfect in itself to allow for any accompanying virtues.

Ella Morris was in the midst of a sociable chat on the Stall family when the girls came into the house. Ella never failed to gloat over her intimate knowledge of this family and was clever enough to know how uncomfortable such conversation made Linda Shirley. Linda hated herself for listening, and yet she could never tear herself away while Ella dwelt on the sacred name.

"Mrs. Stall was saying only today how Courtenay couldn't bear to eat cranberries. Why, she says, a rash comes all over his back. I said she'd better use that salve of mine, and she said she would. She's been poorly herself. Will was telling me last night. It's her organs. Oh, Will says, she does get those terrible pains. Fie, I says, if she's that bad you ought to be home this minute instead of hanging around me! You men, I says! Well, he got as red as a beet. I see you're on to me, Ella, he said. I just had to laugh . . . Did you hear us laughing in there? It must have been after ten."

"I didn't hear you," Linda said with cold restraint. Dorrie looked at Ella reflectively.

"Every time I see Courtenay Stall from now on I'll wonder if he's got that rash on his back," she commented. "And probably every time I see Mrs. Stall I'll think of her organs."

"Dorrie!" Linda said sharply.

"Aunt Jule'll have to speak to that young one," Ella said disapprovingly. "The idea!"

She frowned at Dorrie, and then her eye lit with a newly recalled item.

"Mrs. Stall says Courtenay's running around with some fast girls from Columbus," pursued Ella. "She doesn't know what to do. Send him to me, I said to her. I'll give that youngster some good advice."

Youngster! Linda recoiled at the impudence of it!

Ella was about to describe the way Mrs. Stall kept Courtenay's woolens from shrinking, but here Linda forced herself to go on upstairs. She was to help Mary James with a cider and doughnuts party in the basement of the Lutheran church that evening, and she had to change her clothes.

The party proved to be a dull, unsatisfactory affair, as most of Mary's parties were. There were a lot of fat, country girls, and a half dozen gawky country boys in enormous white collars and squeaky new shoes. Linda smiled sweetly through it all, and at the end of the evening assured each of the gauche lads that he couldn't see her home because someone was meeting her. Romance she craved, yes, but there was only one person in the world who spelled romance to her, and if he did not seek her, Linda was content to go her way alone. Whether he ever looked at her again, she belonged to Courtenay Stall.

Linda came home alone, as usual, hurrying down the dark streets, her head bent in thought. How she despised Mary James! She hated to have to look to that drab person for her social life . . . Perhaps she despised her for going around with Jule Shirley's granddaughter!

The town clock struck eleven as Linda turned into Elm Street. She quickened her pace at the tracks, for the darkest stretch lay there along the birches. Tonight she saw an automobile in the shadow of the birches. Its lights were off, but she could see a slouched figure at the wheel. She hurried a little, not because she was afraid but because she hated being seen alone late at night. Ladies do not roam about at midnight without escorts. Better alone, though, she thought, than to be seen with one of Mary's rural heroes!

She noted, with a little annoyance, that no one had left a light burning for her. Even the hall light was turned off. At the porch steps, she stood still an instant, for she caught a glimpse of a girl coming around the house from the back way. The girl did not see her but tiptoed across the lawn toward the street.

"Hussy," muttered Linda under her breath, as she recognized Esther Mason. "How dare she go out this time of night!"

She deliberately stamped her feet as she went up the steps.

That would show Esther that someone had seen her.

"O-o-oh, goodness!" squealed a voice from the depths of the porch. "I didn't see you, Linda. My, how you scared me!"

"Why, Ella!" exclaimed Linda, peering through the gloom in complete bewilderment.

"Sh-h! Don't let her hear!" hissed Ella. "Who was he?"

"Who was who?"

"Who did she meet?" impatiently elucidated Ella. "Here I've been sitting for just hours waiting to find out who she was going to meet, and then he never came up to the house at all. Who was that waiting down by the birches? I thought I saw a car drive up there."

"No one there when I passed," Linda said, her lip curling in disgust at Ella's feverish curiosity. She'd die rather than give her any satisfaction.

Ella gave a petulant cluck.

"I declare that's mean," she said aggrievedly. "I was dead sure of catching them. Here I've been sitting ever since she talked to this party on the phone. I had no idea he'd be this late, but I guess with married women you've got to play safe. Hee, hee! You know," she giggled, "I was sure it was old Mr. Remer. Can you imagine?"

"Don't you think I'd better wheel you into your room, Ella?" asked the girl.

"Oh, I suppose there's nothing to see now," sighed the invalid. "If you don't mind giving me a lift...You're sure, Linda, there wasn't a man waiting for her down there? Because I know just as well as I know my own name that she was going out all night with some fellow from town."

"I didn't see anyone," said Linda, wheeling Ella into the house. An icy thought for the moment numbed her heart. A sudden remembering of those slouching shoulders in the car down by the birches... Then she banished it as quickly as it had come, before it had even become articulate in her mind. She was quite tranquil when she spoke to Ella again.

"Do you want your sleeping tablets, Ella?" she asked.

"No use," snapped Ella Morris. "I won't sleep a wink anyway."

* * *

For many weeks, Linda Shirley's head was bent low when she walked down Birchfield's main streets. Everywhere it seemed voices were whispering. "Aunt Jule's house . . . Esther Mason . . . Esther Mason . . . Claire Moffatt . . . Claire Moffatt . . . Mystery . . . Scandal!"

"Did you hear? Did Ella tell you? Claire Moffatt has come back to Birchfield and is staying at Aunt Jule's place! Ella says she has foreign labels all over her trunks! She says she's recovering from an operation, and all she does is lie around the room! She says Claire is terribly rich now and her husband's picture looks as if he was some New York broker or something. She says Jule takes her in a tray of breakfast every morning . . . She says she's changed . . . Too bad her folks are dead because they'd certainly be glad to see her if she's as reformed as Ella Morris says she is."

"But if she's reformed, what is she doing at Aunt Jule's?"

Thus did Mrs. Remer and Mrs. Stall and Mrs. Eph Miller discuss her who was to Dorrie the loveliest lady who had ever come to Birchfield. It was the main item in all poolroom conversation in Birchfield. Even in the second Wednesday dances of the Birchfield Country Club, the women gathered in the dressing room to speak of Claire Moffatt's return, and the men in the smoking room mentioned it in a significant undertone.

If Claire Moffatt, once the bad girl of Birchfield, had returned the same Claire as she had been ten years ago, nice people would not have referred to the matter except to show concern over the danger confronting their young men. But the flamboyant painted little hussy of ten years ago, who had run around the streets night after night with the equally bad Nettie Parsons from Mansfield, had returned to her hometown a suave, exquisitely groomed lady whose only offense so far had been to room at Aunt Jule's instead of the Birchfield House.

"She's married well," Birchfield said, adding with justifiable bitterness: "When you think of what she was ten years ago and how easy she got a rich husband, it makes a person disgusted with men! Why, look at the good girls in town who are old maids! Yes sir, a girl might better be bad if she's looking for a rich husband."

"She always was a clever one, though," Mrs. Eph Miller said, reminiscently. "I remember when I was teaching, she was always giving smart answers. Different, you know. But she was had!"

Yes, the gracious beauty in Aunt Jule's front parlor had certainly not paid the wages of sin. She had run away from Birchfield ten years before and the citizens, confident that she had gone definitely to the bad, were amazed to hear a year or two later that the Moffatt girl was writing her folks from Paris. The Moffatts were a good family, and the whole town had been sympathetic over their unfortunate choice of offspring. But at last the girl had reformed.

"Blood tells in the end," the Birchfield ladies said to Mrs. Moffatt when that tired little woman showed the Paris letter. After that, they heard of Claire's marriage to a wealthy New Yorker, a honeymoon in Venice and Egypt—beautiful clothes, jewels—and then Birchfield heard no more, for the Moffatts both died and Claire had no other mouthpiece in Birchfield for her progressive adventures.

"We really ought to call on her," Mrs. Remer said to Mrs. Stall. "For dear old Mrs. Moffatt's sake we ought to forgive her."

Birchfield was ready to forgive anyone who became successful. The result was that Ella Morris found herself with a rival in Jule's house for the town's attention. She made jealous comments to Jule, while Claire Moffatt graciously received her one-time enemies in Jule's front bedroom.

"I'm not going out," she told them, in the lovely foreign voice she had cultivated, and which enthralled Dorrie. "You see I've stopped here just for a tiny rest."

"A negligee with fur on it!" Mrs. Remer reported to the Browning Club.

"A closet full of evening gowns!" Mrs. Stall added.

"Her eyebrows are pointed and thin like actresses', but I don't think she pencils them!"

"Just because she seems rich, people think she's turned into a lady," Ella jealously complained to Jule. "She used to be a lot worse than Esther Mason when I was a girl. She's as old as I am, too, even if she does try to get herself up like a chit. If she tries to say anything to me, I'll just up and ask her how it feels to be thirty-two."

"She's wonderful," sighed Dorrie. She could think of no one she'd rather be than the mysterious scented lady in the front room. Pale, mauve nightgowns . . . Rose satin mules with black French heels . . . Cobwebby underthings in delicate rainbow tints, trailing out of two huge trunks . . .

Enormous photographs of princely men crowded over the old oak dresser . . . Vials of opalescent magic . . . Faint clouds of perfume floating in the lovely lady's train . . . Long banners of Italian lace flung over the dresser and chiffonier . . . An iridescent pink taffeta coverlet across the walnut bed . . . A gorgeous purple and gold Spanish shawl tossed on the big, square table and a gold-lacquered box placed on it . . . "Chinese influence on Spain," Claire had commented to Dorrie.

The front room became a dream paradise to Dorrie. She sat at Claire's feet, wordless. The old scandal concerning this adorable creature did not trouble her. She naturally remembered nothing of it and Ella's allusions never really meant anything. Claire was a princess, poised for a moment, in this unworthy spot . . . And Dorrie tried her hand at a series of sonnets in her praise.

Even though Birchfield had tentatively decided that Claire was to be forgiven for her errors of a decade ago, Linda refused to warm to her grandmother's new lodger. She *had* been bad once, and that was enough for Linda. Furthermore, the whole town was talking about her, and Linda shrank from further prominence for Jule's lodgers. She bowed to Claire distantly when the guest wandered into the kitchen to beg for hot water, but a bad girl was a bad girl, in Linda's eyes, no matter how thoroughly reformed.

"Why is she here, anyway?" she tersely demanded of Jule. "Where is her husband?"

"He's in Bermuda," Dorrie replied. She was getting old enough to resent Linda's slurs on her idols. "And she's come back to her hometown to wait for him. She's been ill and wants to rest."

"Indeed! . . . If she's so rich, why does she stay here?"

"Because," Jule put in softly, "I'm the only real friend she has in town. Ten years ago, even . . . My, she was such a pretty, pert little thing!"

"Yes, you would be nice to her at her worst," answered Linda, sarcastically. "If you ask me, I think she's here because she wants to show off before the town, and maybe see all her old beaus! More than likely she hasn't any money left."

"Oh, Linda, you're horrid!"

Dorrie left the room when Linda talked about her violet-eyed goddess. She could not bear to hear such doubts cast on Claire's perfection. You couldn't stop Linda, though, so you had to go away and shut your ears.

Claire was just past thirty. She had a tawny brown slender white face—a startlingly red mouth. She wore sleek satins that enhanced the supple curves of her body, her tapering thighs. When she slept—and Dorrie had watched her sleeping—her long black lashes spread lacy shadows over her marble cheeks, and you were positive her eyes, when she should open them, would be dark. It was thrilling to watch the lids lift drowsily to reveal deep violet pools . . . Courtesans learn many things. Claire, the ignorant, provincial girl, had acquired in her long career of yielding a patina that only sin can give. She was authentic. And authenticity makes courtesans and duchesses equal . . .

Perhaps there were times when Claire thought a little quizzically of the brazen little painted girl who had caroused behind the railroad buildings with the toughs of Birchfield a long time ago. What a pity! . . . What a pity when the thing could be done in perfect taste with no damage to one's self-respect as Claire had since learned . . . Perhaps she felt a little sorry for that girl she once had been . . . But one had to learn . . .

"Poor women," Claire must have thought, looking at fat Mrs. Miller and tiresome Mrs. Remer through her half-closed eyes. "Poor women."

In her few years of discreet misconduct, she had learned the gestures of a woman of the world. Socially she was ten times more eligible than the virtuous ladies who called on her. After all, when had virtue ever taught a woman anything? Virtue could not give a woman culture. Virtue could not make a woman beautiful. Virtue could not make a woman happy . . .

Birchfield speculated as to what had reformed Claire Moffatt. Was it marriage? Was it simply maturity? Or was it wealth? Birchfield wondered. At least it was her rumored wealth that had helped them to forgive her.

Dorrie went in shyly every morning with coffee and toast for Claire. She put the tray at the bedside while Claire's slim, curved body stirred gently under the taffeta cover. A white arm pushed slowly upward and arched above the tawny brown hair on the pillow. The eyes opened. The lips parted in a luscious, sleepy smile.

"Dorrie, how good you are to me," she would yawn and sit up, leisurely piling the pillows behind her. She would reach silently for her foamy pink negligee, and Dorrie would give it to her. Then she pushed her hair back over her white, delicately veined temples, gave Dorrie another delicious, amused smile, and began to sip her coffee.

They said very little. Dorrie could think of nothing to say to her, and Claire did not believe in conversation. But Dorrie knew that here was the woman she would like to be . . . a mysterious, scented creature with a silky charm . . . If only she had blue eyes!

Claire was a Catholic. Each Sunday morning she dressed in an irreproachable black costume and went to mass. Dorrie spoke to Jule about becoming a Catholic, too, but her grandmother was alarmed at the idea. The Shirleys had always been Unitarian. Ella hastened to tell a story of a nun who was locked in the wall by priests. Dorrie said nothing further on the subject to her family but vouchsafed an awed inquiry to Claire concerning this mysterious "mass."

"I'll take you next Sunday," promised Claire. "Be sure and be ready. Perhaps if we get up early we can walk over by the river road."

Dorrie was breathless with anticipation. She hinted of it to Jule, and Jule hurriedly changed the subject rather than deliver another warning on Catholicism. It bothered her too much.

Sunday morning Dorrie was up early, eager for the first sound from Claire's room. She rapped on the door but no one answered. Disconsolately, Dorrie went back to the kitchen and waited a little while. It was early. Still Claire had mentioned walking over by the river road and that was nearly two miles. Dorrie ended by going back and rapping again on Claire's door. Getting no answer, she softly pushed it open.

A queer stench assailed her nostrils as she opened the door. The shades were drawn and for a moment, Dorrie, perplexed, blinked in the dark room. Even in the darkness she sensed something strange and fearful about the room. Confusion, somehow, and that queer, nauseating stench that came out of saloon back doors . . . Dorrie rubbed her eyes . . . Bottles on the table and the Spanish shawl crumpled up on the floor. Dorrie held her breath . . . Sprawled sidewise on the bed lay Claire, blowsy, stertorous, her negligee disheveled, her hair tangled over her face—and beside her was Tim Cruger. Even in sleep his mouth leered. His boots made muddy marks all over the pale taffeta coverlet.

Dorrie rushed out of the room, numb with horror, her eyes smarting.

"It isn't true—I didn't see them—I didn't see them—I didn't see them—" she told herself, desperately. She was dreaming. Oh, no, it couldn't have been. Tim Cruger!

Dorrie scurried up to the attic and sat in a huddled, forlorn little heap in the garret storeroom next to Mr. Wickley's. It was not true. Things weren't like that. Oh Claire, Claire—lovely lady!

Dorrie stayed upstairs for a long time. Was it a matter of hours or days? She could not have said. When she came down it was because she heard Claire's voice calling her name. She was standing, impeccably gowned in black, at the foot of the stairs, faint blue shadows under her eyes the only signs of her debauch.

Dorrie was so ashamed for her that at first she dared not lift her young stricken eyes.

"Run for your coat, dear," Claire said gently. "Did you forget we were going to mass?"

* * *

"Women that are bad once are always bad," Linda Shirley said about Claire. Dorrie had not told anyone about that Sunday morning, but when Linda said this, the tears rose to her eyes. She could not banish the picture of Tim Cruger's leering face and muddy boots on the rose taffeta cover.

"She smokes cigarettes in her room," pursued Linda somberly. "You can always tell by that."

Dorrie said nothing.

"Oh, I know she has all the airs of a real lady," Linda granted. "But I wouldn't trust her for minute. Did you hear what Ella said? . . .When she asked to see a picture of Claire's husband, Claire showed her that big one on her dresser. But she told Grandma it was the one by the door in the gold frame."

"Maybe she married twice," Dorrie faltered. She remembered the day she had shyly admired the foreign officer whose photograph stood on the broad windowsill.

"Do you like him?" Claire had said idly. "That's my husband, you know."

Linda's lip curled at Dorrie's naive suggestion.

"That's not the worst. Those men weren't either of them her husband. They're movie actors. One was Maurice Costello and the other Harold Lockwood. That one in the foreign uniform in the window is the crown prince of Romania! She lied, that's all. She forgot which one she had told Ella when Grandma asked."

Dorrie looked out the window. Her throat ached with controlled sobs. She would never, never forget that Sunday morning. Her lovely lady! If it had only been Maurice Costello instead of Tim Cruger! And if only she hadn't looked so soiled. She could scarcely say a word to Claire that day. She didn't want to look at those violet eyes. Beautiful ladies should sin beautifully.

"Two bad women in the house," Linda said. "How many more must Grandma have before the police raid the place?"

Dorrie was startled.

"What's more, that Claire woman hasn't paid a cent since she's been here," Linda went on. "I suppose if she really were decent, Grandma would put her out . . . If she's so rich, why doesn't she pay her debts?"

It was only a few mornings later that Ella Morris wheeled herself into Jule's kitchen, her tongue delicately moistening her lips as if in preparation for a feast, her black topknot at a triumphant oblique angle, her eternal tatting in her lap.

"Well!" she exploded, noting with honest pleasure that Jule and Dorrie and Linda were all present, seated about the kitchen stove. A full house . . .

"Have you taken Claire her coffee yet?" she asked Dorrie.

"She told me not to bring it until eleven this morning," said Dorrie, sensing calamity in Ella's pleased face. "Why?"

"She did, eh?" Ella, repeated, smiling a little. "See that you don't forget it then, my girl. If you knew what I know, though, you wouldn't bother about that lady's coffee today."

"What is it, Ella?" Jule was standing by the sink, drinking her midmorning cup of coffee. She held the cup for a moment before her lips, eying Ella uneasily. "Do speak out."

"Claire Moffatt's gone," announced Ella.

"What!"

"Went last night," delightedly explained Ella. "Ella! Quick, Dorrie, run up to her room and see!"

"That's right—call me a liar . . . Well, sir, I'd just like to see Mrs. Will Stall's face when I tell her the young lady she thought had gotten so cultured had run off in the middle of the night. Why, she sneaked off like a regular thief!"

"Owing you thirty-eight dollars board bill," Linda said accusingly to Aunt Jule.

Jule put her cup down on the sink. Her eyes were gentle and a little sad.

"I wish she'd told me she was going," she said, meditatively. "I wanted to mend that blue silk petticoat of hers. She was all for throwing it away but I told her a few stitches would make it good as new. I could have done it in ten minutes . . . I wish now I'd taken it and done it when I thought of it."

"Oh, Grandma, you haven't a bit of common sense!" Linda cried. "Mending petticoats for women who are trying to beat you out of your money!"

"I could have stitched it up in no time," mused Jule regretfully.

Ella gave an impatient cough.

"Well, don't you want to hear how I found out?" she asked petulantly. "It was this way. The 4:10 to Cincinnati woke me up this morning. It always starts to whistle way up in Cleveland, I guess, and keeps it up all the way down the line. I've a good notion to write a letter to the paper about it . . . I reached over for my tonic, and I thought I could see Bert, the baggageman, standing under the light out in front of the house. Well, who's going away this time of night that they have to have help with their trunks, I said to myself. Then next thing I heard a noise in the hall like a step, and I see Claire running across the lawn with two suitcases. He took the baggage and she ran on ahead."

"What about her trunks?" Linda demanded.

"I looked in her room as I passed," Ella said. "Not a stitch left. She must have had him take her trunks over just afore I woke up. Mighty sly, I call it."

"What are you going to do about that money, Grandmother?" Linda asked. "That shows you what she is, and how little she appreciated all you did for her."

"She didn't mean any harm," Jule said patiently. "She must have let it slip her mind."

"Do you suppose she didn't have any money?" Dorrie asked anxiously. She felt a little sick from Ella's news. "Maybe she didn't have enough to buy a ticket."

"Poor thing," sighed Jule, pouring herself another cup of coffee, "she must be in real want."

"Nonsense!" said Linda. "She's just a bad woman without any sense of honor. All her fine clothes and manners couldn't change her. It's just as I said at the very start. A bad woman's always bad . . . bad clear through."

Dorrie sat in the corner and said not a word. She was remembering a white arm arching lazily above tawny brown hair.

Chapter Four

Miss Bellows was a short dowdy little woman who wore her round sailor hat on the back of her head. Long wisps of black hair were continually blowing about her fat, rosy face. The perspiration dripped from her forehead when she played the piano, and she breathed heavily during the difficult passages.

Liszt was her favorite composer, but teaching "Sleigh Bells" and "Shepherd's Dance" soon took that out of one.

She was having a hard time establishing herself in Birchfield, and she spoke finally to Aunt Jule about giving up the "studio." It was after supper, and Jule's small family was in the front room, again the parlor since Claire had left.

"If I could only get one of the nice girls from East Walnut Street," Miss Bellows sighed, standing before the little gas heater and staring with worried eyes into its puny flames. "It gives you such a standing to have Walnut Street pupils. But my goodness, Miss Lundquist just has everybody that's of any account in this town. And here I thought I was going to make a lot of money in Birchfield! Harold is a junior now, you know, and if I can just get him through I don't care what happens."

Harold was the brother Miss Bellows's savings were sending through college.

"You get Gertrude Stall and you'll have the whole raft of them," Ella Morris said. She reached slyly in her crochet bag for a chocolate. Mrs. Remer had brought her a box last week and Ella didn't think it would be fair to share it with anyone. She usually carried three or four in her handkerchief and disposed of them without ostentation.

"I wish I could get her," sighed Miss Bellows.

"No use, Miss Bellows," said Ella, kindly, taking up her work again—a doily for the church fair. "Miss Lundquist is in good health, and so long as she is, Birchfield's going to stick to her."

She emphasized this with a smile and a nod. Miss Bellows bit her lip and was silent.

"They'll come to you yet," Aunt Jule encouraged. "There's not one of them can say a word against you, and that's the thing that counts in the end."

Linda coughed.

"So long as she stays here they'll talk," she said in a low voice. "You know that, Grandma."

"About me?" Miss Bellows asked in wide-eyed anxiety. Her round eyes filled with indignant tears, which she winked back steadily. "I'm sure I've always done what's right. Goodness knows I've always worked for a living, and it's hard for me, too. You'd be surprised how much it takes to clothe a growing boy, let alone put him through college."

"Birchfield thinks you're bad just because you live in the same house with bad people," Linda said indifferently. "You should have had your studio someplace else."

Miss Bellows's small plump form stiffened a little. "I guess I can manage to live down whatever they say about my living quarters," she said tartly, "if that's all. Let them just give me their trade."

Aunt Jule wiped her glasses at this manifestation of loyalty.

"Linda's not feeling well lately," she apologized. "She doesn't really mean that bad people stay here. She just feels a little low."

"Maybe it's her teeth," suggested Ella Morris hopefully. "I shouldn't be surprised if a trip to the dentist would improve her whole system. My! What a change in Mrs. Remer since she's had all her teeth out. She's a different woman."

"I suppose you think I ought to have mine pulled," Linda said with grim amusement.

"We-ll, you never can tell," Ella retorted.

Miss Bellows stood in the doorway. If her hair had been tidier she might have looked like Queen Victoria.

"I'll keep the studio another month anyway," she said to Aunt Jule. "I can afford to do that much."

Aunt Jule rose and padded after her.

"If you can't, you know," she whispered, with a quick apprehensive look at Linda, "it'll be all right—you know."

Miss Bellows went back to her own room.

"She'll never get Gertrude Stall," said Ella, her upper lip curled scornfully. "Why, that girl's got talent. When she finishes with Miss Lundquist, her ma says they're going to send her down to Columbus to study with one of those swell teachers. Her ma told me she's going to be a concert pianist one of these days."

"She's too fat to be a concert pianist," Dorrie proclaimed over the back of Shelley. "She'd look terrible in a pink velvet evening gown, and that's what they have to wear."

"Nonsense, Dorrie!" Linda rebuked her.

"That young lady's getting entirely too outspoken, Aunt Jule," Ella advised, with a nod in Dorrie's direction. "I'd speak to her if I were you."

"Dorrie's all right," Jule comfortably assured Ella. "She tells the truth more often than necessary, maybe."

"I don't think that old man upstairs does her any good," Ella pursued, staring reflectively at Dorrie. "She's likely to get funny notions from him. I've heard he's one of these atheists . . . 'Tain't good for Dorrie."

"He won't do her any harm if Esther Mason and Claire Moffatt haven't," Linda drily commented. "You ought to know that, Ella."

"Well, well," said Jule, adroitly twisting the subject back again to safe ground, "so Gertrude's going to be a concert pianist."

"People always clap most for her at Miss Lundquist's recitals," Dorrie stated, "but it isn't because she plays the best. It's just because she's a Stall."

Birchfield was always loyal to its aristocrats.

"Mrs. Stall's taking her to Columbus on Saturday to interview the big music teacher down there," said Ella. "You know the one I mean. Old Professor Whatsisname. Five dollars a lesson. Why, I says, Mrs. Stall, you're foolish to put that money into it. I know, Ella, she says, but the girl may be a genius."

Linda's face stayed a flaming crimson. She knew it got red whenever people talked about the Stalls. She only hoped nobody noticed it, though from Dorrie's intent gaze, she might have guessed that at least one person knew her weakness.

"Poor little Miss Bellows," mused Jule, staring into the fire. "I wish we could make it easier for her, someway. Get some new pupils for her."

Ella Morris worked her jaws spasmodically. She wanted to say that Birchfield had enough music teachers, and anyway Miss Bellows was too up-and-coming for her taste. Unfortunately, she had just set her teeth into a caramel, and so her opportunity passed.

* * *

Linda was ironing her shirtwaist on the dining room table when Gertrude Stall called. It was the morning of Thanksgiving Day, and certainly Linda would never have dreamed of answering the doorbell if she'd thought it was other than the butcher's boy. She had on a frayed old white petticoat and a blue crepe dressing sack whose sleeves were pinned back on her shoulders with great safety pins. She was wearing a pair of purple bedroom slippers. Linda was so careful of her office clothes that she never dreamed of wearing them around the house. Her yellow hair was drawn tightly back and massed on the top of her head in what is accepted among women as the bath coiffure. No, had Linda known it was Gertrude Stall, she would have died rather than answer the bell. As it was she stood in the doorway transfixed, gazing at the plump figure of her goddess. Gertrude was a fat replica of Courtenay, and Linda was furiously ashamed that eyes so like Courtney's should see her in this unbecoming dress.

"Is Miss Bellows in?" asked Gertrude, after a slight nod of discreet recognition to Linda.

"Miss—Bellows?" Linda swiftly took herself in command. "She's in her room. Shall I tell her to come out?"

"I'd rather go to her studio," said Miss Stall.

Linda thought curiously that the girl looked as if she had been crying. Her round face was blotched and her eyelids pink. Her obvious confusion helped Linda in recovering her own poise.

"She's just finished a lesson, so you can go right in."

From Miss Bellows's room came a faltering trail of arpeggios—and then silence.

"Bye, Miss Bellows," said a plaintive voice.

"Don't you dare come next week without knowing your lesson," was Miss Bellows's none too agreeable farewell. The little Crawford girl hurried joyously out and Gertrude Stall entered.

The door closed behind her.

In the hallway Linda stood breathless, bent to catch the explanation of this unprecedented visit. It must be that Gertrude Stall proposed to take lessons of Miss Bellows, and if she came every week to their house, she could not fail to become aware of Linda's existence. She would see then that Linda Shirley was different—that she was a "nice girl."

It was true that Gertrude was changing her music teacher. She had gone to Columbus for a trial lesson with the great Professor Flisk. That great man had stopped her in the very middle of "Arabesque," her prize effort, to suggest another year under a lesser master than himself. He had further suggested that since she lived in Birchfield, there was no reason at all why she should not take of Amelia Bellows, his former pupil and friend. He really did not feel that he could take the responsibility of getting Miss Stall into concert work until she had picked up a few more of the—er—fundamentals of the piano.

The Stalls, somewhat crestfallen but impressed, had returned to Birchfield with a changed program for the talented daughter. Indeed, Mrs. Stall, having seen the look of anguish on the great master's face during Gertrude's performance, had had her faith slightly shaken in her daughter's genius. She had been very thoughtful ever since.

Miss Bellows wormed this pitiful story from Gertrude's reluctant lips.

"How dare she be so officious!" Linda groaned, hearing Miss Bellows's staccato commands and queries. "She'll never come again—never—and Gertrude'll think I'm to blame for that woman's impudence."

She heard Gertrude slashing incredibly through her "Arabesque." She winced in actual pain at Miss Bellows's curt comments.

"She just wants to show her authority," Linda thought resentfully. "And Gertrude will be mad and never come again."

Miss Bellows, indeed, seemed to be thoroughly enjoying her little triumph. Miss Stall would really have to begin all over again, her foundation was so poor. Miss Stall had a ridiculously advanced repertoire for a pupil of her elementary capabilities. Miss Bellows could not consider teaching Miss Stall unless Miss Stall would place herself absolutely in her teacher's hands. They would simply have to begin all over again—from the very beginning. Yes indeed, the girl's foundation was quite hopeless. Absolutely.

"I lit into her," Miss Bellows confided later to Jule. "It was a treat. Goodness knows I ought to have kowtowed to her after the way I've been crying for a swell pupil, but—well, I just felt like putting her in her place. I was a fool, but that's the only pleasure a poor woman has—being a fool once in a while."

When Gertrude finally emerged, her face was flaming and her chin quivering but held high. In the downstairs hall Linda stood, having hurried into her gray poplin. The indignant guest brushed past her without a look.

Linda stood for a moment, sick with her eternal disappointments. Miss Bellows had had it in her power to bring the Stalls closer—to make Linda's dream clearer—and the woman, the hateful selfish woman, had rejected it. She had driven Gertrude Stall away, never, never to return. Hereafter the great family would look with even more aversion on all the people at Jule's place.

"It's not fair! It's not fair!" Linda cried. She leaned against the wall, her blue eyes brooding on the departing figure of the Stall girl. She twisted her fingers until they hurt. She saw Miss Bellows come down the hall, her hair straggling over her forehead, her cheeks flushed.

"Now you've done it!" Linda flared. "You wanted her so much, and when she came you insulted her. You drove her away. She'll never come again—never—"

"I don't care if she doesn't," snapped Miss Bellows, taken aback at Linda's outburst. "That's my business."

"It's mine too!" Linda said in a white heat. "They hate me already, and now they will blame me for your insults instead of you. I'm the one who will suffer for it."

"I don't see what there is to get hysterical over," Miss Bellows retorted. "Don't talk nonsense, Linda."

Linda shut her mouth tightly. Always someone set her dream crashing at moments when it seemed most near. This was what life would hold for her forever.

"What in the world possesses you this morning, anyway?" Miss Bellows asked, with more curiosity and less resentment. "You don't have such spells often, I hope. Just because I wanted to put that stupid girl in her proper place."

Linda made no sound for a moment, just standing there against the wall, her hand at her throat as if to choke back the words that might betray her.

"There's no use explaining things to you, Miss Bellows," she said finally in a low restrained voice. "You wouldn't understand."

She fled upstairs to her room. Miss Bellows looked after her, her brows knit.

"Hm . . ." she said thoughtfully, "I'm not so sure."

* * *

Three times during the following week Linda met Gertrude face-to-face on the street. Each time, Gertrude stared blankly through her, and Linda knew that she had sunk deeper in the Stalls' regard because of Miss Bellows's desire to "put that girl in her place."

"They think Miss Bellows has been boasting to us of the way she got the best of the Stalls," Linda thought moodily. "Gertrude doesn't want to let on that she cares."

But the next Friday Gertrude Stall came again to Jule Shirley's house. And she came once a week thereafter. The Stalls began to brag about how hard it was to get lessons from Amelia Bellows. Actually, even Gertrude had to prove her talent before this temperamental teacher could be persuaded to take her! And Professor Flisk had as much as said she was the best teacher in Central Ohio.

"Miss Lundquist was getting a little common," Mrs. Stall whispered at the Five Hundred Club. "Teaching everyone in town, you know. Miss Bellows takes very few pupils—very few."

"But do you think it's quite all right for Miss Gertrude to go to that house?" asked one of the ladies. "George says all the riffraff from the trains stop there. Fast women and gambling men, and even crazy folks, I've heard."

Mrs. Stall found herself obliged to defend Aunt Jule's in order to protect her own daughter's name.

"That's mostly talk," she said, with an indulgent smile. "Aunt Jule herself is a really fine character, Ella Morris says. And Senator Morris would never allow his niece to stay any place that wasn't absolutely safe . . . Oh, Gertrude's quite safe."

She decided, however, it might be well to convince Miss Bellows of the necessity for other quarters.

"One of the stupidest pupils I've ever had," Miss Bellows observed to Aunt Jule, anent Gertrude. "But, oh my! She does bring the business with her."

Linda resumed speaking relations with Miss Bellows after this, but she never wholly forgave her for that interview with Gertrude until the day Courtenay called.

Again Linda went to the door, but this time she had just come in from the office and had not yet changed her office serge. He stood slouching against the porch railing, his checkered cap pulled jauntily over his eyes, and his hands in his pockets. He wore the dirty old leather and sheepskin jacket he had worn all through Purdue.

"Ma wants Gert to bring Miss Bellows to supper when the lesson's over," said the young man. "Gert expects me to get the car out and take them over, but you tell her there's too much snow. Besides, I'm busy . . . Well—bye, Linda. You fix it up."

He smiled quickly at her and then swung off whistling. It was the longest conversation they had ever held. Miss Bellows was to be thanked for it, for it was all due to her giving lessons to Gertrude. Linda forgave her everything then, and at Christmas gave the little music teacher three hemstitched handkerchiefs with Linda's own lilac sachet on them. Miss Bellows was greatly touched and Aunt Jule very proud and happy.

* * *

At Christmas Aunt Laura sent a box of her cast-off clothes for Linda and Dorrie. The distribution of these yearly boxes was usually a simple matter, for Dorrie invariably wanted the beaded frayed elaborate things, in which she posed graciously before the mirror but for which she seldom found practical use, while Linda chose simple serge things which could easily be made over. This year there was a yellow organdy party dress with scalloped flounces and a cluster of lavender ribbons on the shoulder. It must have belonged to Margaret, Laura's only daughter, but as soon as Linda saw it she knew it was meant for her. She was not vain, but she instinctively knew that the style and color would enhance her own formal blonde beauty.

"You could wear it to Mary's Valentine bazaar in the church," Dorrie suggested helpfully, well pleased with the stained green velvet she had fished from the bottom of the box.

Linda smiled faintly. She would never tell Dorrie, but this was the dress she would wear to the Birchfield Country Club Ball when her day came.

Courtenay spoke to her often now. Linda lifted her eyes to the stars and dreamed lovely perilous dreams.

* * *

Aunt Laura wrote a letter to Aunt Jule, inviting Linda to come down to Columbus for two months.

"She's not a bad looking girl, and it's high time she was getting married and off your hands, Mother. My Margaret knows a great many young men from the university and the town, and Linda would have opportunities, I am sure. We would arrange for her wardrobe, or, for that matter, she could wear Margaret's things perfectly well. Really, Mother, I'm doing this to take her off your hands for a while. Dorrie is such a vulgar disagreeable child I should hesitate to relieve you of her, but I shan't mind Linda, and she'll be company for Margaret.

"I was thinking the other day how annoying it would be to have the family connected with any of those ghastly Birchfielders, and something ought to be done to get Linda out of there now that she's almost twenty and probably thinking of marriage. I should never forgive you if you were to let her marry one of those bumpkins . . . Only the other day I ran into Alma Stall in the streetcar, here in Columbus, and had all I could do to keep her from calling on me. Impossible people! I was annoyed at her *nerve,* when you remember that only fifty years ago her uncle was Grandfather Shirley's coachman. Well . . . let me know when Linda will come. I assure you, Mother, it will be for the best."

* * *

"That's very nice of Aunt Laura," said Linda, struggling with bewilderment at the last part of the letter. What queer things Aunt Laura said about the Stalls. Still . . .

But she didn't want to leave Birchfield. She could not keep her still vigil over her lover if she were sixty miles away. She did not want to offend Aunt Laura, the respectable wing of the family, but—

Jule unexpectedly tossed the letter into the stove.

"Don't you go," she said, with the perverseness she always showed toward her two prosperous offspring. "Like as not she wants you because you're pretty and Margaret's not, and you'll bait enough young men for both. That'd be just like Laura."

"Nonsense, Grandmother," said Linda. "I'm sure Aunt Laura meant to be nice . . . Still, I'm afraid I ought not to go. Mr. Fitz said he was going to raise my salary to eight dollars a week next month. I ought not to give up a good job like that."

"Certainly not," Jule heartily agreed. "It would be the worst mistake you could make. A good job like that! Good jobs don't grow on trees, I can tell you. You sit right down and write your aunt. Don't let on I influenced you."

Jule dipped her hands into the dishpan and started vigorously scouring pans. On her tender sensitive mouth there played a smile of malice, and a perverse twinkle gleamed in her eyes. Linda sat down to reject the opportunity to win a wealthy husband as casually as she had dismissed the love-smitten baron. To Linda, no family could be more desirable than the Stalls, even in the capital city, no man as dazzling a catch as Courtenay. She had no desire to be impersonally envied by women all over the States for some brilliant match she might make. For her, the definite envy of Lucy Remer, Francis Riggs, Molly Miller—Birchfield. Her triumph must be one of intensity rather than scope—a triumph over tiny Birchfield, the town that had known her degradation. She wanted to show them—but she wanted her triumph to be always before their eyes; she wanted to enjoy it the rest of her life—to satiate herself with their groveling respect.

***

Aunt Jule was getting really worried about Lew Mason. Lew was such a clumsy lout it was hard to feel sorry for him, but, as Jule told Ella, you couldn't help but feel worried when a fat man begins to lose.

"Why shouldn't he?" Ella commented amiably. "Look at his wife. Enough to wear a man to a shadow, worrying about that wanton."

"Ella! When she's behaving herself so nicely now," rebuked Jule. She was darning Linda's stockings with deft old fingers. "Why, she's been as ladylike and quiet as a heart could wish for ever since last fall. Not a misstep. Don't you think she's done well, Miss Bellows?"

"Oh, I guess the girl means all right," Miss Bellows said absently. She was cleaning gloves on Jule's kitchen table. You couldn't have that gasoline smell in your studio, what with all the young swells calling for lessons there. She wasn't listening much to Ella's chatter. She was really thinking about raising her fee to seventy-five cents a lesson. Thirty pupils at seventy-five cents a week—

"Maybe she's behaving and maybe not," answered Ella Morris. "There's talk."

Here Miss Bellows awoke sufficiently to say that there'd always be talk so long as some folks had tongues in their heads.

"You may mean somebody in particular by that speech," said Ella coldly. "But you don't mean me because I'm not a talker. I don't say I don't listen. That's different. But what I hear I don't tell, except to my dearest friends."

Miss Bellows observed that it must be wonderful to have so many friends, and with a dry significant cough left the kitchen. Ella sent a baleful look in the direction of her retreat.

"Lew's worried about his wife's extravagance, like as not," she resumed to Aunt Jule. "She used to be pestering him for money every minute. Oh Lew, I'd hear her going on in there, please let me have eighty-five cents for that remnant over at Keller's. And probably the very next day it'd be—Oh Lew, I've just got to have some change. Can't you let me have a dollar and a half? I'll be awfully careful . . . Poor man didn't know where he was half the time. People don't make money in the livery business the way they used to."

Jule shook her head.

"But she doesn't ask for anything anymore," she said slowly. "Seems like the less she asks the more he worries."

"He looks more like a bloated fish than ever, now that he's lost thirty or forty pounds," Ella ruminated. "Goodness, those waggly eyes of his! All bleary and horrid! They just look like—well, do you know what they remind me of? Grapes. Grapes with their skins off."

Ella smiled with the true artist's pride in this neat figure.

"They don't fight anymore," Jule pursued reflectively. "I don't hear a single cross word."

"Maybe that's the trouble," Ella suggested.

"There's always trouble when married folks stop fighting. Shows they're holding something in, and that's bad."

Aunt Jule made an extra apple pie and sent it in that day at noon. Lew was having his lunch alone, for Esther was taking her weekly trip to Galion to see her cousin. Lew's legs were so fat he always had to straddle a chair, and that pushed his stomach way up, making breathing an arduous labor. The loss of twenty pounds had somewhat mitigated this unfortunate condition, but heavy breathing had become a habit now, and after each speech he was apt to sit panting for several moments.

He lifted forlorn eyes to Jule. They swam about wanly in their red-rimmed sockets. He sat at the oilcloth-covered table, one fat hand encircling a glass of beer. The other was busily conducting great chunks of bread and cheese to his mouth. He stared gloomily at the steaming pie which Jule set before him.

"She's a bad 'un, Auntie," he muttered hollowly. "No use talking or saying any different. Won't I turn her 'cross my knee good and proper today when she comes in? Wait . . . You just wait."

Jule paused in the doorway.

"Esther's just as true as steel," she said firmly. "Don't you get any fool notions into your head, Lew Mason. You know you married a girl young enough to be your daughter. You have to treat her like one."

Lew inserted a wedge of pie into his mouth. His mouth being full gave a sepulchral note to his words. "She's a bad 'un, Auntie, I tell you . . . She's bad."

Chapter Five

Spring brought the usual train of transients to Jule's. Drummers, theatrical folk, and, once, a traveling Italian band, for whom Jule converted both parlor and kitchen into a dormitory and dragged two extra folding beds down from the attic.

"I do wish I could ask Mr. Wickley to double up with one of the men," she sighed. Dorrie discouraged the suggestion.

Still, the musicians didn't mind sleeping four to a bed and three on the floor. And if it hadn't been that the manager neglected to pay her, Jule would have made ten dollars for her trouble.

In May, Doll Darling came. Doll was really a distinguished guest if you looked at it reasonably, for she was own daughter to Major Darby Darling, Buffalo Bill's most dangerous competitor. Doll had had a long and stormy career as snake charmer in the Darling Circus, but a recurrent malady—which she designated as galloping consumption and others called delirium tremens—obliged her to give up her art. She stopped off at Jule's until her daughter, who lived near Shelby, several miles distant, should get back from California. Then she planned to spend her old age benignly knitting mufflers for her daughter's babies. She even hinted at a dear little cap with lavender streamers, but that was being sentimental.

Jule had discreetly tucked the lively old lady into the back bedroom on the second floor, and she was there a good three days before Linda realized that another subject for scandal was in their midst. She compressed her lips and sent slow resentful glares toward Jule—glares which Jule blithely pretended not to see.

Dorrie could not refrain from boasting a little at school that they had a snake charmer right in their house—indeed none other than the far-famed Doll Darling herself! The town was amused and disgusted by turns as this news traveled.

Doll was a thin bony hag with coarse gray hair screwed back from her skinny old face into a tight topknot. She had wild startled eyes and a nose tilted upward to the point of being nothing but a petrified sniff. From morning to night she wore low-cut gowns of imitation silk studded with imitation jewels. They were skimpy bedraggled things, invariably dipping in back and hitching up over the stomach. They exhibited a scrawny, wrinkled neck and shoulders above, and a pair of skinny, withered legs below, with feet encased in slender pointed brown shoes, the toes of which turned up at the same alert angle as her nose. For streetwear Doll usually wore over this costume a sailor's pea jacket and a pancake hat draped with two exhausted willow plumes. Jule herself laughed a little at the old lady mincing along the street in this remarkable garb.

"Daughter will put me in black alpaca and a lace bonnet when I get there," Doll confided to her. "I might as well get the good out of my wardrobe while I'm here."

Doll carried with her in her travels a small black chest which she kept under her bed. Dorrie was positive it contained snakes and in a bold moment peeked in. No snakes were there, although the half dozen bottles of brown fluid probably had venomous potentialities. Dorrie disappointedly gave up her idea.

Doll would occasionally oblige, however, by invoking imaginary serpents from the closets and corners of the kitchen after she had been stimulated by a pleasant hour or two with her corn whiskey. On such occasions she would leap and whirl about Jule's kitchen like a mad dervish. It was truly a spectacle, and Dorrie used to sit in fascinated horror, watching the old lady's picturesque cavortings. But never was the old snake charmer more enchanting than the night of Linda's triumph, the night when her dream came true. History was made in the old black house that night, and Doll Darling played the most important part in it. It was a night of horror for Linda Shirley, a night that she dreamed of for weeks and weeks after the thing had actually taken place.

Ever since Gertrude Stall had started taking lessons of Miss Bellows, Linda had risen inch by inch toward her far-off goal. One day Courtenay stopped her on the street to ask her if she'd tell Gert to tell Ma he wouldn't be home tonight. Next day he would nod to her from across the street. Linda trod a path of stars, slowly forgetting the handicap of her home, living for each new sign.

At night she stood at her window, looking over the birches with luminous eyes. Her day was coming! Oh, never had it seemed so near!

And it did come!

On the morning of May Day, Linda had hesitantly put aside her blue serge and winter coat and resolutely donned her white serge coat over a light blue foulard. She got out the little pale blue taffeta turban which Aunt Laura's box had held and found that it fitted her head. More than fitted—it marvelously became her fair hair and shell-pink cheeks.

"I should save it for Sundays," Linda thought, guiltily, looking with surprised pleasure at her image in the mirror. "But now that I pass Courtenay almost every day . . ."

She met Courtenay that very morning at the corner of Main Street. The snow had just melted and the air was delicious. The streets were bathed in tremulous sunlight. Linda was a radiant picture, walking under the leafing trees. A part of spring, she seemed.

Courtenay's cigarette dropped from his fingers at the sight of her.

"Oh, it's Linda," he grinned. "Gee!"

Linda blushed at his obvious admiration and walked on. It seemed unbearable that such a bit of loveliness should vanish, and Courtenay, searching his stupid brain, hit on the first thing he could to hold her.

"Say—er—Linda," he called, and then walked up to her. "What are you doing tonight?"

Linda's eyes became bluer. Her teeth caught her lower lip in an effort at control. She stared helplessly at him.

"I thought we might go for a ride or something," he amplified.

Linda started to speak but her voice seemed gone. "I—"

"Oh, come on," he urged, affecting nonchalance. After all there wasn't any sense getting all fussed up over the Shirley girl, even if she was pretty. Why, he actually felt afraid of her—afraid she'd freeze him—him, Courtenay Stall! He threw back his shoulders. Catch any Birchfield girl turning *him* down! "I'll drop around about eight."

"But tonight," Linda quavered, "is the May Dance at the country club. I thought—"

She meant to add she thought he would be going there, but he construed her unfinished sentence otherwise.

"Oh, that's so." He was thoughtful. "You mean you'd rather go there? Well . . . let's go there, then."

He had forgotten that May Dance. Now it struck him as an amusing bit of bravado to take an "outside" girl there—one of the Shirley girls. She was pretty enough, so he didn't care what his mother and the other folks said. After all, what was the good of being the social leader of the young crowd unless you could get away with whatever you liked? The thing appealed to Courtenay.

"Oh—I—yes, I can go," Linda articulated. "I—I'd love it."

"See you at eight, then."

He was gone, his tall, lounging figure in its red and black blazer a part of the poolroom furnishings for the day. Linda, winged with joy, flew on, her heart dancing madly.

The dream was coming true! She did not eat supper that night. She said in a muffled voice that she was "going out" and hurried up to her room with a pitcher of hot water and fresh towels for a bath.

Oh, she would be beautiful—beautiful! She scrubbed her straight white body and powdered it with lilac. Linda's body was slim and hard. Her breasts were white and firm, her delicately tinted flesh as unyielding as marble. Youth without resilience . . . beauty without warmth . . . Silks and soft gracious things would never have suited her as did her starched white linen underthings and her crisp yellow organdy. The cluster of soft lavender ribbons hanging from the shoulder lent a touch of delicate yielding charm. Linda, obscurely irritated by it, was half-tempted to take it off.

She spent a full hour on her long yellow hair, with the latest fashion magazine beside her, turning to "Modish Coiffures for the Debutante." High on her head made her neck look too long, she thought. Figure number four showed the coronet of braids, but that was the way Mary James wore her hair. She finally wore it coiled gracefully on the nape of her neck.

"Linda," came Dorrie's excited voice at the door. "Courtenay Stall's downstairs. He says he's taking you to the May Dance. Is it true? Oh Linda, please let me in!"

Linda opened the door.

"Oh—Linda!" Dorrie gasped, looking in wide-eyed reverence at her sister's radiance. "Oh!"

She sat down on the bed, open-mouthed and awestruck.

"Don't act silly," Linda admonished in some embarrassment.

She tried on the white serge coat, disguising the elation in her eyes at the mirror's flattery.

"Gee, I'll bet Gertrude will stare when she sees you there," Dorrie declared proudly. "Everybody for that matter."

Linda's eyes became miserable for an instant. She didn't want Birchfield to stare. Conspicuousness was the thing she dreaded.

"Don't you use my room while I'm gone," she said with a final glance in the mirror. "You used all my notepaper, and there's no use your denying it."

"Oh, Linda, don't be mean," Dorrie begged, "when you look so beautiful."

She stood at the head of the stairway while Linda went down, and heard Courtenay's low whistle when he saw her.

"Gee!" Dorrie thought, "this is Linda's night, all right. Ella Morris will feel awful when I tell her where Linda went and who she went with."

Linda did not utter a word all the way over to the Elks' Hall. Courtenay was not a true gallant, and rather than give his lady any undue praise which might make her "cocky," he affected to be oblivious of her appearance after his first spontaneous ejaculation. But within he was gloating.

"She's a daisy, all right," he was thinking, with masculine pride in his discovery. "But oh, boy, won't the folks be furious when they see us! Hope I can carry the thing through. Hate messes with Ma and Gert."

His daring in the face of Birchfield opinion was more than repaid when he caught the low whistle that ran around the men's cloakroom as Linda passed. Courtenay realized that he was envied by all his friends, and his chest swelled. The girl was a peach, if you didn't know who she was.

Linda caught that murmur too and knew what it meant. Her color heightened. It was all a dream, for it was thus that all her dreams had run.

Murmurs of admiration—herself in a beautiful gown, the center of all eyes . . . soft music . . .

The hall had been festooned with colored paper streamers and the Elks' Property Box lanterns, which were for Halloween really but were used for all festive occasions, obscured the glare of the electric lights. At one end of the hall a three-piece orchestra sat, wearing white flannel pants as a concession to the country club. It was a Columbus orchestra for this May Dance, although the club was usually content with Miss Lundquist at the piano, Chester Riggs at the violin, and young Carl Hodges at the drums. The players exchanged light chatter with friends among the guests, and the leader ran a trained eye over the assembling crowd to determine which girl he would play to all evening. He picked a new girl tonight, a glowing blonde in yellow organdy, who appeared to be with young Stall. . .

The punch bowl stood on a table before the Cozy Corner, where hung panoramic pictures of the "Elks' Picnic at Ruggles's Beach, July 1907"; "Elks' Picnic at Cedar Point, July 1908"; "Elks' Picnic at Casino Park, August 1910"; "Elks' Picnic at Ruggles's Beach, July 1912"; "Elks' Picnic at Luna Park, August 1913."

Here Mrs. Harold Remer, as wife of the president, presided in a pink silk shirtwaist, gold watch with fleur-de-lis pin, and a black satin skirt. Assisting her was little Lisbeth Remer, age twelve, a very fat little girl bulging in the most unfortunate places, in white ruffled dimity, her hair done up with a pink ribbon forming a huge rosette just above one eye. Mr. Remer, benignant in his dress suit, welcomed one and all at the door, quite as if it were his own private party.

He was so taken by Linda's fresh beauty that his face showed acute pleasure before he actually placed her. Even recognition could not dampen his delight in this visitor. He liked a pretty girl as well as the next one!

"How could I have thought they were snobbish," ran through Linda's intoxicated mind as the men clamored for her dances and paid her clumsy compliments. Then she went into the dressing room, and the cool unfriendly stare of the women reminded her of her effrontery in essaying to climb the slippery social ladder of Birchfield.

"Men are much more broad-minded than women," she thought. She wished a little for Mary James when she found herself sitting alone occasionally between dances while the other girls collected in high-pitched giggling groups around the punch bowl. But as soon as the music began, half a dozen men would start sliding toward her from as many ends of the ballroom. Perhaps tomorrow their wives and sisters would scorn them thoroughly for their exuberance, but a pretty girl was all too rare at the Birchfield dances to allow one to wither merely because her grandmother kept a shady boarding house. After all, young Stall had brought her . . .

Courtenay was as attentive as he dared be, but the horrified steady eyes of his mother and the reproachful averted eyes of his sister made him a little more uncomfortable than he had expected.

Once, in the hallway, his mother caught him as he was hurrying out for a smoke.

"Oh, Court, how could you do it?" she murmured sadly. "The whole town's talking. What will your father say?"

Courtenay shook her hand away angrily.

"Take who I damn please," he muttered, and pushed on.

Each time Linda saw him coming toward her, she caught her breath in sharp ecstasy. One instant more and his arms would be about her, her own resting on his. It was not the thrill of physical nearness so much as the thrill of possession. Here was the person who symbolized what she wanted most to own, and for the space of two stanzas and a half dozen repetitions of a chorus, she owned him. For that brief spell, Jule's house did not exist, nor the shame of sinning lodgers. Linda knew happiness.

What did a few rude women matter—a few whispers—hostile feminine eyes? They would be conquered in time by the force of the Stall name.

"He likes me," Linda thought. "He pressed me so tightly. He looks at me as if he thought I was pretty. When he bent over and kissed my arm there in the shadow . . . I hope he didn't see how I hated that . . . He likes me. Perhaps—"

It was madness to think of it, but such mad things were happening all the time. Who knew where they would end? She could see the other men congratulating him, and his boastful swaggering acceptance of their compliments. He was proud of her. He was glad he had brought her.

Once Linda had asked nothing more of life than to be permitted to go to the country club dance—just once, and to dance only once with Courtenay. Now that more than this had been granted her, she saw another vision before her, and a further goal.

"Heard somebody say you were the prettiest girl ever here," Courtenay briefly commented as he led her through the steps of an old-fashioned schottische.

Linda was a correct, if not an inspired, dancer. It bothered her a little to have Courtenay hump his shoulders and lean over her in the fashion then prevalent in collegiate circles. But she looked light and exquisite in the fragile organdy frock, and, to the envious old wives sitting 'round the punch bowl, as to the "stags" smoking in the hallway outside, she seemed a golden autumn leaf blown lightly by the wind.

Triumph. At last Linda took her cloak from the dressing room, so flushed and absorbed by her conquest that the hostile silence of the women did not penetrate.

Her night!

They walked slowly home. Linda was inarticulate with happiness. Things weren't bad at all. Courtenay had showed that he did not mind Jule's, nor her being Jule's granddaughter. And really the place wasn't so objectionable nowadays, since that Mason girl was behaving herself and Claire Moffatt had left . . . Linda's heart sank a little, remembering the snake charmer.

Courtenay was silent too. It seemed queer to be turning south instead of north. Nice people didn't live in the south end. It seemed queer to be escorting somebody to that old house up there beyond the birches. Tonight the boys had applauded him for bringing "a little peach." Tomorrow they would be in their everyday mood. She wouldn't be a peach then. She'd be the Shirley girl. Old Jule's granddaughter. The fellows would think he'd lost his popularity with the buds of Mansfield and Columbus and had to bring a girl from the south end of town. The Shirley girl.

Linda's step lagged as they approached the house of her misery. After her triumph it seemed a black reminder that fairy tales did not happen in this life. Its blackness in the moonlight seemed ominous, sinister.

They passed the birches. At the porch he would say good night. What would he say? Would he ask if he could see her again? Linda's heart quickened in anticipation.

"I've had a lovely time—Courtenay," she said shyly, extending a slender white hand. Her light dress billowed about her in the night wind, and her fair hair blew softly against her cheeks. In the wan glamour of starlight she looked mistily beautiful . . . Courtenay's throat tightened a little, inexplicably. He bent toward her face, his eyes dilated with the sudden intensity of his desire.

"Linda—"

But he never finished the sentence. A horrible shriek split the air . . . Another shriek . . . Dorrie's frightened outcry, and then the thud of a falling body.

Linda tore frantically toward the kitchen, Courtenay at her heels.

Triumph?

That night Linda's heart broke.

* * *

Ella Morris and Aunt Jule had gone to the movies after Linda left for the ball. Dorrie had collected half a dozen books from the bookcase, including *Wormwood*, *Wedded and Parted*, *Père Goriot*, and of course her beloved Shelley. Lodgers were always leaving books, but they seldom left anything worth reading. Dorrie opened *Wormwood* and, shuddering, cast it aside. *Wedded and Parted* she dismissed after the first few paragraphs and the last page. *Père Goriot* interested her. Dorrie turned up the gaslight above the dining table and prepared for a literary evening. She had her pencil and a few pages of Linda's notepaper in the Shelley, in case—as often happened—the inadequacy of other authors would inspire her own muse.

Before settling down she inspected the pantry and found a great crock of sweet pickle and another jar of her grandmother's best pickled watermelon rind. It looked like a very pleasant evening.

She had consumed six plates of watermelon pickle and almost finished *Père Goriot* when the door into the hall opened and Doll Darling's henlike head was thrust out.

"Hello, honey," she whispered, with an air of great secrecy. "Can old Doll come out for a little talk?"

Dorrie put down her book. It was nearly half past eleven—high time her grandmother and Ella were returning, unless they'd stayed for the second show and ice cream at the drugstore.

"Babies got loose tonight," whispered Doll archly. She had on a short black petticoat and a hideously flowered dressing sack above it. Her nose, to Dorrie's ingenuous eye, seemed to be a little feverish tonight. "Can't tell where they're hiding, but don't worry. Doll can always get them back. Takes time. Got to be patient. But old Doll gets them every time. Keep your eye on old Doll, honey. She knows her babies."

Dorrie, sensing that Doll's babies were reptilian, instinctively drew her feet up under her. She looked uneasily at the old woman, who tiptoed with a sly evil smile about the room, peering into corners and winking at Dorrie with a sinister significance. Unexpectedly, she began to chant in a low fearsome voice, crouching before the stove and then leaping over to the closet, charming snakes from all corners.

"See her? See her, honey? Ah-h-h-h-h! Come out of there, you green devil, you slimy bitch! Come out of that oven, you dirty hellion! Doll sees you there—old Doll sees you! Come on! Ah—that's the girl, that's the girl—over to Aunt Doll . . . Look at her, honey! Look at her! She's afraid . . . the she-devil is afraid! She knows—ah!—she knows all right!"

Dorrie sat transfixed on the chair. Her amber eyes grew wide and wondering. Her heart beat very fast. She was afraid. The old hag was as horrible as the boa constrictor she evoked. Her eyes were green and rolling. Her neck was long and scrawny, and it stretched and contracted like a snake's body. Dorrie hated to look at her, but she was horror-bound. Oh, if only grandmother would come in.

Suddenly the snake charmer crouched low, her eyes narrowed and glittering. She took a slow, pouncing step toward the pantry door—lifted her foot high another step, menacing, fearful. She stopped.

"You're there, Bess, all right. I see you, Bess," she crooned. "I told you I'd get you if I caught you lovin' up my snake babies. Think they'll love you better'n me, don't you, Bess? All right . . . Men do, don't they, Bess? Never had any trouble gettin' men away from me, did you, dearie? Just the snakes, you couldn't vamp . . . Well, well . . . Pretty little Bess. Tryin' to get old Doll's jungle babies to love her. Lie down there, you green devils! And you, you black poison! Sh! Sh! Sh! She doesn't see me—she doesn't see me . . ."

Dorrie watched the crouching old monster, her heart thumping. What was in that pantry? What did those horrible old eyes see in that dark closet? . . . Then with a wild yell the old woman sprang into that darkness. Dorrie leaped after her in a panic . . . Green, gold, black slithering snakes were all about her, crawling up the walls, flying through the air, wriggling, sliding, darting . . . Dorrie shook herself to dismiss such ghastly phantoms. She ran into the pantry and stopped just beyond the door. On the floor old Doll sprawled, her head bloody where the shelf corner had gashed it. She lay quiet, gasping. Her green eyes were wide and astonished.

"You know, honey," she moaned wonderingly to Dorrie, "Bess wasn't there at all."

"What is it, Dorrie?" Linda's cool controlled voice came from the kitchen doorway. "We—we heard the scream."

Dorrie looked around, dazed. Linda stood fragile and aloof in her yellow organdy, her face bleak with premonition. Behind her, now amused and curious, was Courtenay Stall, his eyes, with faint scorn, on the dirty kitchen and the bloody old hag on the floor.

Linda's night!

"What is it, Dorrie?" Linda asked again, so sick with the futility of her brief triumph that she could scarcely speak. She dared not look at

Courtenay. If he had forgotten her shameful connections for a little while, this assuredly would make him remember.

Dorrie gulped. She felt sympathetic shame and understanding for her sister. She wanted to smooth things over for her so that Courtenay would not think Linda's home was the brothel it seemed.

"Why, it's nothing," she said, awkwardly, "really, it's nothing."

"That sort of thing happens every day, eh?" grinned Courtenay.

He no longer looked at Linda.

Dorrie flushed and twisted her hands uncomfortably. Linda lifted her head proudly. The dream had gone, she knew—forever.

"Yes, Courtenay," she said, quietly, "that sort of thing happens here every day."

That night she put away the yellow organdy. It was a long time before Linda saw Courtenay Stall at Jule's house again.

* * *

Linda grew pale and thin. Her grandmother looked at her sometimes and shook her head. Life was so hard for Linda. Linda made herself suffer so. Jule was unhappy over Linda's unhappiness. She ached for the girl, sensing the truth. She knew that Linda considered her grandmother the cause of her social degradation, but this did not diminish the old woman's tenderness for the girl. Dorrie was herself—another Jule to be taken for granted. But Linda, beautiful frozen Linda, she loved because Linda could hurt her most.

Courtenay Stall never saw Linda. When they met on the street, face-to-face, he happened always to see someone across the way. Linda, head bowed, rushed on. Doll Darling had gone to live with her daughter near Shelby, but she would never be forgotten by Linda Shirley. An everlasting monument to Doll stood, made of the broken stones of Linda's fallen castle.

Linda had gone to see Mary James again, one night after the party. She hated to come back to Mary James, but she was very lonely, desperately in need of a confidant.

Mary's stuffy little parlor, with its mahogany veneer and green leather parlor set, irritated her. Once she had thought it was very refined, in much better taste than Jule's hodgepodge of oak, black walnut, and cherry. Now, all of it displeased her—the chenille portieres between Mary's parlor and dining room, the stiff cushions—one of leather with an Indian painted on it, one of linen with "A Woman is Only a Woman but a Good Cigar is a Smoke" worked on it, and a Lincoln head on another in green and tan poplin, with "You can fool some of the people all the time . . . etc. . . ." the flourishing fern before the bay window, the colored bead-fringed dome above the dining table, the *Boy with the Cherry*, in bronze, on the piano . . . Marks of discreet prosperity and anxious discrimination in Birchfield. The Jameses had held this parlor as their ideal for years. When they were able to afford it, the style in parlors had changed, but their ideal of luxury had remained the same, so they fitted this one up with tremulous pride. They were working to have a cement porch now. Everyone else had one.

"The furnishings are all right, but they don't look the real thing, somehow," Linda thought, a little puzzled at her own changed reaction. "The Jameses simply don't know—they don't have taste."

Mary was strangely unsympathetic tonight. A faint malice flickered in her bluish-white face.

"I forgot to tell you I went to the Birchfield Country Club Dance," Linda began with assumed carelessness. Perhaps if she told someone about her triumphant moments at the ball, the memory of the tragic finale would be erased from her mind. Mary would tell her how marvelous it was that she had been invited, that she had had such a pretty gown and such things. The glow of that ball's beginning would be renewed in her memory.

"Oh, the dance?" Mary repeated with an odd smile. "I heard about it."

Linda's mouth opened in a little exclamation.

"After all, it's a small town," Mary went on bending over her embroidery hoops. "Things like that get around."

"Why?" Linda asked, too taken aback to disguise her chagrin. "Why should people talk when I go to a party? I'm sure that's not of much importance."

Mary's needle sped.

"Don't forget who you went with, my dear," she said demurely, "and what happened afterward."

"What?"

A cold wind swept over Linda's heart. She stared at Mary's bent head, the tidy little waves in front, the two little snails of hair at the back. Mary was jealous, of course. Jealous because Linda had gone to the party, and jealous again because Linda hadn't told her all about it at once. She was just getting even now. Mary leaned over the dining table—they always sat in the dining room except on party nights—and picked up her scissors. She snipped some threads with maddening deliberation.

"Yes, Linda," she said, and her voice held a restrained triumph, "it was all over town next day. And how, when you got home, one of the boarders was having delirium tremens."

Linda stared at her, speechless. There was open hostility now in Mary's eyes.

"No wonder you didn't tell me about it," she said, laughing a little breathlessly. "I wouldn't have told anyone if it had been me. Right before Courtenay Stall, too."

There was only one explanation of Mary's knowledge. Courtenay himself had told . . . And if he had told, he had laughed—laughed at her. That thought twisted in Linda's heart.

"Have you seen him since the ball?" asked Mary, her pale cruel eyes dancing.

"Don't you know?" Linda flung back, tortured. "I'm surprised you haven't snooped around until you found that out, too."

Mary winced a little.

"Nobody needs to snoop to find out about the Shirley affairs," she retorted. "They're all over town as soon as they've happened."

"Too bad the James's affairs are so dull that no one is even interested enough to talk," Linda thrust in return, clutching the chair with one hand for moral support.

Mary was flushed and excited now that Linda was giving battle.

"You've had the protection of my good name long enough to know there's no scandal in our family," she said, stammering a little. "You've no right to talk that way, Linda."

Linda got to her feet and jammed her hat down on her head.

"I have the right," she said, "but I don't care to use it. You make me perfectly sick, do you hear? Do you understand, Mary James? I don't want to ever see you again. Never!"

Mary wilted. She dropped her embroidery. Tears welled to her protuberant pale blue eyes.

"Oh, Linda," she faltered, "don't, please don't let's quarrel. I didn't mean anything. And I did hear that Courtenay stuck up for you in the poolroom when all the fellows kidded him for taking you. He said you were pretty—only he didn't want a girl with DTs in the family."

"I don't want to listen to you, I tell you—I hate you!" Linda cried.

She rushed blindly to the door and out into the street. Mary James ran after her, flustered and hysterical. But the door slammed back in her face. She sat down on the hall steps abruptly.

"Oh—oh," she gasped, blinking at the door. "Oh—oh."

Chapter Six

Next to Mr. Wickley's room Dorrie loved her attic study best, and if it hadn't been for the rats, she certainly would have insisted on sleeping there. Through the thin walls you could hear the echo of old Wickley's rumbling voice in the adjoining room. But if you were a real poet this did not disturb your creative moments any more than did grandmother's calling: "Dorrie! Dorrie! Where are you? Come and wash your dishes!"

After a while Jule would stop calling. It was a mere pretense at discipline anyway. She didn't mind doing the dishes herself . . . much more peaceful than panting upstairs to face her undutiful grandchild. Dorrie usually frowned a little, pencil poised in air, until her grandmother's voice had died away. It never occurred to her to answer any more than it occurred to her grandmother that she would.

There was only one tiny window in the attic, and in spring the apple tree thrust a blossom-laden branch across this aperture. The petals blew across the floor—rafters in a ghostly flutter. Once Dorrie had stolen up there at night to be alone. Pale blossoms, she saw, making a gleaming haunting pattern over an old trunk. Moonlight quivered over it and trickled into a far corner—was lost in the eaves. The old portrait of Grandfather Shirley, backed against a broken-down chair, caught the light and winked in grave comradeship at Dorrie. The ancient gowns, crinolines, basques, a Confederate uniform hanging on a clothesline across the garret—breathed . . . sighed . . . Certainly that was her own mother's shadowy smile above that brown velvet basque.

Dorrie had stood uncertainly in the doorway, her hand still on the knob. She had meant to sit by the window and brood over things in a rapt loneliness . . . She might even write a poem . . . But the apple blossoms and the moonlight frightened her. She had wanted solitude! . . . Why—the attic was full of people!

Daytimes, Mr. Wickley's voice reassured one.

Then Dorrie sat cross-legged in the floored space beneath the little attic window and wrote in an old brown ledger. It was a simple matter to write a poem. You needed a sharp pencil and a clean page—and then you wrote. That was all . . . Dorrie had been tempted to tear out the ballad about Lady Claire. It hurt too much to see it and be reminded of that Sunday morning before mass. The poem on Phil did not matter. She had renamed it "Sonnet to a Fat Lover," which was one way of being revenged.

"Of course," she reflected, chewing the end of the pencil, "he isn't fat yet, but he will be in ten years. So!"

Life was crowded with disillusions. There was Claire . . . There was Phil . . . There was even Steve. Steve hadn't run away to sea at all. He wasn't going to be an admiral. He was going to own a garage and tinker with stupid automobiles and things. He had proudly told Dorrie of his new ambition. Dorrie's eyes reproached him now, constantly. To have Steve fail her too! She looked at him with a cold, hardened gaze.

"He really is a very dirty boy," she told herself to ease her disappointed achings. "And his ears flop."

Steve didn't know why Dorrie suddenly stopped being chummy. You'd think a girl would be glad you had some ambition and wanted to get away from the livery stable business. He was a bright young man, too, the garage man had told him. Only seventeen, and picking up the business the way he had. But then he was a man now. Every Saturday night he went to one of the bad houses in Mansfield with the fellows. Probably that was why Dorrie

Shirley wouldn't talk to him anymore. It never occurred to Steve that Dorrie could have excused all these things easier than his failing in the adventurous quest of the seas. He'd said he was going to run away to sea and—he hadn't.

A dirty boy with floppy ears!

Dorrie wrote poems about the baron instead. She realized sentimentally that it must have been him she really loved. Alas! She had never known! She reconstructed a beautiful image of the poor little baron—a lithe, dashing nobleman who loved her madly. Sometimes she brushed away a tear . . .

* * *

Mr. Wickley read from a great, dull green book. Dorrie huddled on the window seat.

"I wonder," she mused aloud, "if I am really beautiful, or if I just think so. Mr. Wickley, am I really beautiful?"

The old man lifted sunken eyes in which there played a faint gleam.

"You're beautiful, child," he answered, slowly, "if one admits that the ugly is always the beautiful."

Tears rushed to Dorrie's eyes. Linda always said she was plain, but she herself had known better. But the wise Mr. Wickley . . . A rumble that might have been a vast chuckle issued from the old man's throat.

"What does it matter? Why should you wish to give pleasure to others by your beauty? . . . Enjoy beauty, child. Don't trouble to possess it." He stared at her with expressionless eyes for a moment, then waved his gaunt arm in a sweeping gesture.

"This—this is beauty," he said. "This musty room. These dirty sheets. This rotting old house . . . Sordid, filthy beauty . . . You and I, child, are sybarites . . . and dear Jule."

Dorrie's eyes widened.

"Beauty," the old man rumbled on, "is the mask for decay. Decay is the mask for beauty..."

"But—but—" Dorrie faltered.

"My eyes are too old to see external things," Wickley murmured. "Probably you are very fair. It is not important. The thing that is important is to watch life mirrored in a dark pool, lest you see a reality and be turned to stone."

"Is philosophy a dark pool?" asked Dorrie.

"A dark pool—" nodded the old man, "where things that have no value are given values . . . Poetry is another."

Dorrie's black eyebrows met in a straight line and she frowned studiously.

"The dark pool is inside you, though," she said with conviction. "And when that's so, you couldn't see a Medusa if you tried."

Again the deep rumbling sound that might have been a chuckle. Dorrie looked up, a little startled.

And then over the parched old face came a troubled shadow . . . He fumbled under his pillow and drew out a letter.

"Some will find beauty in death," he said slowly, "but that is not so sure."

Dorrie watched him unfold the letter. Perhaps it was from Roger, though she could see it was not a Cambridge postmark on the envelope.

Mr. Wickley only held the letter in his yellow trembling hands a moment, and then dropped it to the floor.

"War," he muttered. "What nonsense!"

* * *

There were weeks now when Esther Mason did not show herself even once in Jule's kitchen. You could hear her moving about on the other side of the partition, humming softly or engaging in monosyllabic conversation with her husband. If Jule tapped on the door to present her with a plate of freshly baked doughnuts or a jar of preserves, Esther was cheerfully grateful but brusque. If she caught sight of Linda over Jule's shoulder, a quick sly light came into her eyes and her mouth twitched. But outwardly her conduct was irreproachable. Ella and Jule agreed that the girl had certainly toned down in the last few months.

"She knows how to be a lady," Jule approved.

"Of course there's no telling what she does under cover," Ella admitted, with characteristic cynicism, "but I'll say this for her, she's careful about it, and that's all a body can ask. I suppose that's what you mean by acting like a lady."

Esther's high color had died down, too, living in the sunless little quarters she did, but to Dorrie's observant gaze her eyes seemed more shining than ever. And sometimes, when Dorrie dropped into her kitchen, she smiled the slow veiled smile of a woman who guards a dark, lovely secret—who cherishes vague sins and fantastic delights.

And then, one night, the carnival came to town. The mountebanks and troupers were all sleeping in tents, else Jule would most certainly have accommodated them. As it was, she sat in her carpet-seated chair and fretted that her broken arches wouldn't permit her to stroll down to the fairgrounds and watch the fun. Dorrie lay on the floor reading, not too absorbedly. Upstairs in her room Linda sat and brooded over unhappy things. Through the wall could be heard the restless movements of Esther Mason, after the first fanfaronade of parading bands. Suddenly, she appeared at the door, flushed and wild with suppressed excitement, and beckoned Dorrie mysteriously.

"Don't say a word," she whispered, as Dorrie came over. "I'm not supposed to go out tonight—I promised Lew—somebody else, too—ha! ha!—but I don't care. Let's go to the carnival. I'm dying to. Come on, let's sneak out this way. Sh-sh!"

It was all spread out over the fairgrounds down by the Birchfield River. You could hear the insane music of the carousel from far up the street—hollow, soulless, strident. Then the creaking of the machine and the giggle of a farm girl astride a wooden camel . . . Nearby the Ferris wheel revolved gracefully, and high up a lady squealed. Her man's callous conquering laugh echoed hers . . . Strange, oddly dressed people—mostly rural—walked about, eating popcorn, gravely bearing grotesque dolls and balloons, staring at the sideshows, mumbling innuendoes at the living statues before one tent, or casting hopeful glances at tittering groups of bareheaded town girls.

Dorrie and Esther stood at the top of the hill studying the spectacle for a moment. They exchanged an enchanted glance, and then Esther took Dorrie's hand with a little laughing, breathless cry, and they ran dizzily down the hill.

"Gee, this is going to be fun," Esther breathed.

"Oh, it is, it is!" agreed Dorrie, excitedly. "Do you suppose we're too old to ride on the merry-go-round?"

"Sure—come on!" recklessly cried Esther, "and after that—"

"I'm afraid of the Ferris wheel," Dorrie said. They elbowed through the mob to the carousel. They were conspicuous in their light summer dresses, and Esther had a rose in her black hair and a string of enormous red wooden beads about her throat. At the ticket window two men in pepper-and-salt suits lounged and winked at Esther. She giggled and nudged Dorrie. They rode on the horses, Esther shrieking with laughter, giddily clutching the horse's neck. Indeed, Esther was so noisy that

Dorrie looked apprehensively up the hill lest the echoes had brought out Linda.

"Hope my old man isn't around here," Esther breathed humorously in Dorrie's ear.

Magical, beautiful carnival night!

Dorrie dodged handfuls of confetti and ran to the tent of living statues for shelter. Just beyond her the beautiful creatures draped in a yard or two of cheesecloth, with marble muscles and unwinking eyes, braved the lewd eyes of the crowd . . . all except the little thin one on the end, who had to cough every minute. She had consumption, and the night air was cold, but what could a girl do? . . .

"I want to go into the crazy tent," Dorrie whispered to her companion, but to her surprise, Esther was nowhere to be seen. She looked anxiously around her. When she had run from that storm of confetti, she must have lost her. Dorrie started back through the crowd again.

"Oh, Dorrie!" she heard her name called.

Esther was standing by an auto at the edge of the driveway, talking to two handsome strangers in a touring car. "What do you say to our taking a ride?"

Dorrie clasped her hands. She'd only ridden twice in an automobile. Here were strangers, too—dark, hypnotic-eyed men in dashing ulsters and soft hats. Romance! Romance!

Esther sat in front, and Dorrie, trembling with excitement, sat in the back.

"Let's drive over to Ashland," suggested the man with Dorrie. They whizzed down Main Street, the air blowing Dorrie's hair about her face in scampering curls. The night was very black—there was no moon— only the lights from their car painting a long white way before them. The car flew over this as though on the wind's own back. Horses and young colts leaned over pasture walls to see them, and then galloped off with frightened neighs. Dogs, sleeping before lamplit farmhouses, woke up to bark. A rabbit hopped frantically across their path.

"Fifty miles an hour—pretty good for the little boat," the driver voiced laconically. The speed slackened a little.

The man they called Jerry dropped an arm casually over Dorrie's shoulder. It terrified her a little, but apparently it was merely a gesture to accompany his singing. He sang in a nasal tenor of piercing sweetness:

> Ro-o-oses b-loom for-a-lovers,
> 'Neath the-a sky so b-lue.
> In-a-each petal ho-o-overs
> Honey-a-wet with de-e-ew.
> Faint-a-heart is the stronger
> Under-a-that per-fu-ume.
> Love-a-will lin-ger lon-ger
> Where the ro-oses bloom.

It was somehow thrilling—that cloying voice through the night air, with trees and dark fields sweeping past. Dorrie throbbed with the pain of appreciation. Oh, it was agonizing for life to be so madly beautiful, so carefree—whirling through night with echoes of haunting music in one's ears . . .

Suddenly the car came to an abrupt stop under some low-branching trees. The song stopped too, and Dorrie felt a wet tobaccoy mouth pressed on hers. A nausea of fear seized her. She pushed him back. Even in the darkness she could see Esther and the other man slip quietly off into the weedy fields . . . Dorrie sensed tears rolling down her cheeks. Arms tightened about her. She was small and slight and still with terror . . . Then she struck at him numbly.

"Regular little scrapper, aren't you, dearie?" he whispered in pleased surprise. "Not like your little sidekick with Chet."

"Let me go—let me go!" Dorrie's strangled voice came from the depths of his shoulders.

He laughed conqueringly.

"Regular little scrapper, eh? . . . Why . . . why . . ."

His eyes peered, startled, down at her . . . He put his hand unbelievingly against her face . . .

"Why . . . why, the kid's crying. Say now . . . oh, I say . . ."

In that instant Dorrie sprang out of the car and ran desperately up the road. Black as pitch it was, with no stars. He was behind her, too, in another moment.

"God . . ." Dorrie prayed inarticulately, her legs automatically speeding her on. "God . . . God . . . please, God . . ."

Behind her—the heavy resolute footsteps of her enemy. Dorrie's breath came faster and faster . . . her nails dug deep into her swinging clenched fists . . . her hair fell over her shoulders. . . and still the tears wet her cheeks . . . On . . . on.

The moon rose.

The beat of her flying feet on the cement road and the menacing clop-clop of her pursuer's. Around them the air was full of echoes, echoes of carnival music, carnival laughter . . . A drop of rain fell on her face . . . Confetti.

"Stop for God's sake," she heard him panting. "I can't keep this up all the way to Birchfield."

She ran the faster, but the bridge was ahead and she had forgotten that step. She fell. His arms lifted her up.

"I'm not going to hurt you," he said, as the moon showed her horror-stricken face turned toward him.

"Then—why did you follow me?" she panted accusingly.

"Well, I couldn't have you going home alone on this road, could I?" he cried exasperatedly. "Good Lord, girl, you're five miles from town! What do you think I am?"

Dorrie said nothing. He trudged along beside her, his hands in his pockets, his hat tilted at a swagger angle over his insolent dark face.

"There's a streetcar a mile up here, I think," he said cheerfully. "We can take that."

He looked sharply down at Dorrie's young tearful face.

"You ought not to be out with that girl, you know . . . Why I never guessed but what . . . well, I'm a gentleman, you know. But how was I to know you weren't in her class? Huh? . . . Why, good Lord, look at you! You're only a baby! And traveling with that Mason slut! Damned woman ought to be horsewhipped!"

Dorrie breathed a great sigh of relief at his reassuring sympathy. She walked slower. Far down they could see the lights of the little streetcar station. Terror left her.

"Would you mind," she asked, "singing—you know—that song about roses?"

Chapter Seven

Jule sat the rocker under the oak tree and shelled peas. Spring had come again and the smell of the new grass blew through the air. Jule reflected that this year she really would have to have a flower bed. Nasturtiums and sweet peas and pansies and sweet Williams.

"I say, Ella," she called out without turning around. "Won't it be nice to have sweet peas climbing up your window?"

Ella's room was the corner one on the parlor floor—right behind the porch. She sat in the window in her wheelchair watching people drive past.

"No use, Aunt Jule," she answered in mild amusement. "You always plan a flower garden, and you know yourself that the only things that will grow on this lot are elderberries. They grow wherever there's garbage."

Ella tittered here and closed the window. Jule's mouth tightened with resolution. She'd speak to Tim the first thing tomorrow about planting flower seeds. How they would brighten up the lawn! If the judge were only alive he'd know how to make them grow. He was always one for snipping and cutting in the garden. People had come for miles to see their flower garden on the farm. He never paid much attention to the truck patch—Jule had done all that, but his asters always took a blue ribbon at the county fair.

Jule's hands became still for a moment. The county fairs! They had lived for them in those days. The spring wagon would be hauled out of the carriage barn for this annual festival. Jule would wash it herself with little Jerry and Laura hanging on to her apron strings.

"I'm glad I saved him all those dirty things," Jule thought for the hundredth time. Let folks say what they would, she couldn't have her lord demean himself by scrubbing carriages and hoeing beans. He, the splendid oracle whose mighty words were sought by dozens of dignitaries from all over the state. There weren't many who could remember the old judge now . . . He had died eighteen years ago. And having retired so early, too, from his career. He couldn't stand the traveling. He loved his farm. Six hundred acres! Each year they sold pieces of it. Children had to be clothed and fed, and all the important visitors as well!

Jule dipped her hand absently into the peas. Down the street, Tim Cruger's slouching figure could be seen but Jule did not call to him. She had forgotten about starting the flower bed.

She was a girl now, slim, misty-faced. People had called her the beautiful Juliet Marsh, but Jule had forgotten how she really looked. She only remembered the judge had stopped short that day they met on the church steps . . . It was only a little while after the Marshes had come north . . . She had on the lavender and rosesprigged taffeta, a lilac bonnet with roses caught in its streaming ribbons . . . Her hair, golden like Linda's but drooping in demure curls on either side of her glowing face . . . And he in his black frock coat and white beaver hat, swinging his long cane.

A fine figure of a man was the judge, with his great, broad shoulders, ruddy beard, and flashing blue eyes. *She* had dropped her prayer book, all a-flutter, at the admiration in the great man's eyes.

"Your prayer book, Sister!"

He had bowed very low in returning it. Then, as she was almost inside the church door, that low voice in her ear:

"I know now why I have been coming to church all these years."

Jule remembered the peas again and shelled a few pods slowly, a faint smile curving her lips. It was better to have the memory of the beautiful things he had said to her than to have a memory of his drudging for her. It was better to have toiled as she had toiled to keep his regal dignity unsullied.

He had sat in the high-backed chair before the great fireplace, dispensing wisdom to reverent visitors from far villages come to hear Judge Shirley talk—while in the kitchen his wife mopped. It was not slavery, though, as they said, but service—the service due royalty.

"I couldn't have borne it if he'd had to go out and work with his hands," Jule whispered to herself out under the oak. "I wanted to keep the picture of him that way always—a sort of king."

Jule's hands had never been saved, but they were beautiful hands. They stirred the peas absently. The Shirleys had wondered why she gave up the farm when the judge died. As if so much as a tree on it belonged to them anymore. Not that that part mattered to Jule . . .

She had come directly to Birchfield Village and taken the old house by the railroad. Nobody could say she hadn't made a good thing of it. Maybe it wasn't the sort of work the judge would have liked for her. Maybe not. But there hadn't been much choice. She was all alone. Laura and Theo married and Jerry roaming the globe . . . She had loved it, too, after those thirty hard, lonely years on the farm. And nobody could say she hadn't lived a good respectable life. Nobody. She was respected by all.

"I've had a very happy life," Jule thought, shaking the dreams away and busying herself with her pan of peas. "A very happy life."

She saw Mr. Remer striding down the road, probably on his way to the new waterworks.

"Good morning, Mr. Remer," Jule called pleasantly. "A fine morning."

Mr. Remer nodded briefly.

Jule found herself humming an old camp tune. Oh, it was splendid to be old and remember things. A long, happy life. And now another spring. She must speak to Tim about the flower bed. Nasturtiums and sweet peas and asters.

She saw Mayor Riggs passing now with the surveyors going out to the factory lot. A real good man, Tetlowe Riggs.

"Good morning, Mayor Riggs," she called again. "A fine morning."

"It is, indeed," said the mayor.

Mr. Riggs was very broad-minded.

* * *

Miss Bellows never got any new clothes. It bothered Jule to see her going about in that shiny black suit and battered old sailor, year in and year out.

"It does seem as if she could run down to Columbus and buy a new suit," she commented to Ella as they sat on the front porch after luncheon, "now that she's got so many pupils. It would do her good to primp a bit."

"She's making every bit of twenty-five dollars a week," declared Ella. "Maybe thirty, because goodness knows how much the church pays her for playing the organ."

"Now just see that," Jule ejaculated. "Why, she could buy new clothes as well as not. She's too modest about herself, that's all. I'll have to say a word to her about folks expecting her to look a little more stylish now that she has such lovely pupils."

Ella munched a mint as secretively as her jaws would permit. There was only one layer of candy left in her last box from Mayor Riggs, and after all, he had bought it for Ella Morris, not for Jule Shirley.

"It's that brother of hers," she said presently. "He just takes every cent she can spare. I heard her tell Mrs. Wright he was graduating this year. Guess he had to have a dress suit."

"That's it," Jule nodded. "She says he's a very bright boy. He'll be worth $5,000 a year to anybody when he graduates, he wrote to her the other day. She told me. Then she can spend every penny she earns on herself."

"Hm," was Ella's comment. She cautiously inserted another mint in her mouth.

"Miss Bellows is a very fine little woman," Jule stated, nodding her head by way of emphasis. "Think of it—doing all that for her brother."

"She's a fool," replied Ella succinctly.

The appearance of the music teacher herself put an end to the discussion. She came slowly across the lawn, a letter in her hand, her hat set indifferently on the back of her head. Her petticoat showed a frayed inch as usual.

"We were just speaking of you, Miss Bellows," was Ella's sprightly greeting.

Miss Bellows looked at her dazedly. She lifted heavy feet up the steps and sank into a green wicker chair.

"Warm day," Ella advanced sociably. "June'll be here 'fore we know it."

Miss Bellows looked straight ahead in silence.

"I said it looked like a little shower before night," Ella said, this time a little louder.

Miss Bellows merely sighed and mopped her forehead with a handkerchief.

"I was saying, Miss Bellows," Ella was becoming annoyed, "that the roads are so bad the farmers can't get in today."

The music teacher did not reply. Ella leaned toward her, her long ruddy nose quivering a little with gathering irritation.

"Miss Bellows," she demanded, "aren't you well?"

"It's the sudden heat," soothed Jule.

Miss Bellows blinked then and turned toward the cripple.

"I—I don't know what to do," she said helplessly, and a large tear rolled down her nose.

Ella studied her in some disapproval. Ella disliked things she did not understand, and she certainly did not understand Amelia Bellows at this moment.

"Well, I'm sure I can't advise you," she said. "At least I can't without knowing what ails you and you don't pay attention to what's said to you."

"It's Harold," abruptly explained Miss Bellows.

"I knew it," Ella retorted with satisfaction. "What was I just this minute saying, Aunt Jule?"

"He's not going to graduate after all," went on Miss Bellows in little gasps. "He cheated in his examinations and they—they've expelled him."

"Expelled him!" Jule repeated indignantly. "The idea!"

"After all you've done for him, too!" Ella was shocked and laid a large hand across her bosom to indicate this emotion. "I knew that boy wasn't any good. Whenever you see a woman working her fingers to the bone for some man or other, you can take my word for it he's no good. That's the kind women always pick to slave for."

"Harold isn't such a bad boy," Miss Bellows mourned. "I don't know what got into him."

"Maybe it isn't true," suggested Jule. "He was so bright. These professors don't like to have the young men know more than they do."

"No," Ella Morris said ironically. She looked at Miss Bellows with ill-concealed contempt. Women were forever making such ninnies of themselves.

"Anyway, you can spend your money on yourself now," she chirped. "Aunt Jule and I were just saying you needed some new clothes."

Miss Bellows looked at her blankly.

"She isn't listening to a word that's said," Ella thought, and then aloud, "I hope you've washed your hands of the young man."

Miss Bellows smiled wanly.

"Oh, he still needs me, poor boy. There's a new car out—the Zippy Six—that's going to give him a chance. Another boy got expelled at the same time, and if they can put a couple of thousand into the business, the man's willing to take them into the firm. Harold wants me to go up to Akron next week and see about it."

"Well, I just hope you're not going."

The music teacher straightened her hat thoughtfully. She ignored Ella's remark.

"If I could see my way clear to borrowing the money," she mused, "I could get the 8:10 Tuesday—but I haven't any security."

"There's this house," Jule said in a low voice, instinctively looking over her shoulder to make sure of Linda's absence.

Miss Bellows looked at her with helpless gratitude.

"Such a fine chance for him," Jule pursued, her golden eyes glowing with sympathetic pride. "It's a real opportunity . . . We might go over to the People's Bank and speak to Mr. Miller."

"Oh dear, I ought not to let you." The teacher hesitated with a sidelong glance at Ella's disapproving face.

"You'll be tied up for the next ten years," the latter commented briefly, endeavoring in vain to send a warning glance to Jule.

"It'll be such a fine chance for the boy," Jule repeated in all sincerity. "I'm sure Mr. Miller will let you have it if we explain about this house."

"Hm . . . You'll never see that money again," Ella burst out indignantly. "Nor this house either, Jule Shirley. I'm surprised at you."

Jule stood up and took off her gray percale apron, hanging it over the porch swing.

"My feet don't bother me so much today . . . Guess I can walk along with you," she said tranquilly to Miss Bellows. "Don't mind Ella. She doesn't understand things. She isn't old enough."

She descended the steps slowly and Miss Bellows followed, carefully avoiding Ella's baleful eye. Ella watched them walk across the lawn. As they turned toward the town proper, she snorted. She gave the wheel of her chair a vicious push that whirled her around back into the house. She couldn't hold her indignation another minute. Women were perfect fools. And next to that Bellows woman, Jule Shirley was probably the worst one in the world.

* * *

Old Mrs. Fox stopped off a few days at Jule's on her way to the poorhouse. Her nephew and his wife were moving east and there wasn't anything to be done with her. She wanted to see Jule Shirley, though, before she went. She used to live on the farm next to Jule's. There was nobody like Jule, she thought, though she hadn't seen her since she moved to the city.

She was a wiry little woman of about seventy. She had on her best black moire with the pearl brooch at her jabot. She wasn't going to let those poorhouse folks think she came because she had to. She was going to wear her lavender bonnet, too. She'd been saving it for nearly ten years for a really worthy occasion, and this was her chance.

"You're lucky to have a fine son and daughter," she told Jule, "to look out for you."

"Pooh," scoffed Jule. "If I had had them to depend on, I'd have been in the poorhouse long ago. They'd like me to give up taking roomers so as to be dependent on them. Then if they picked up and moved East like your Myra did, where'd I be?"

"Your grandmother used to be a fine-looking girl," Mrs. Fox told the girls. "She was the belle of this county. Folks used to come from all over the state to see Juliet Marsh. Linda here looks a little like you, Jule. But the little one has your eyes, and your hands, too. Kinda yellow eyes—wide and excited, always, as if they were seeing things nobody else saw."

"I guess Dorrie does," Linda laughed.

Jule wanted the old lady to stay in Birchfield, but the other shook her head. She was afraid of Linda, and Linda had made her position quite clear. As for Dorrie, she looked at Mrs. Fox with mute, pitying eyes. Poor, poor old people. It was terrible to be so old.

One morning, the wagon from the poorhouse stopped at Jule's door, and Mrs. Fox pecked at Jule's cheeks in jaunty farewell. Two bright spots burned in the withered old cheeks, and her small bright eyes were shining with tears. But her head in its lavender bonnet was held high as she tripped down the front walk to meet the wagon. Nobody was going to think she was going to the poorhouse because she had to. The authorities would see that she was a real lady, too. She had Mr. Fox's lodge emblem on.

"Goodbye, all," she called shrilly, waving her handkerchief to Jule and Ella on the porch. Then she looked up at the driver. He was making a place on the seat for her. Something tightened in the old body, and her breath seemed gone. She pretended to be counting things in her bag while the man waited for her to get in.

"Oh, Mrs. Fox—"

At Dorrie's voice, the old lady turned eagerly.

"I'll come and take you away someday," Dorrie said breathlessly. "You'll see. I'll graduate this spring, and then I can look out for you. Don't you worry."

The old lady clung to Dorrie's hands with tremulous fingers and then resolutely she climbed up to the seat in the poorhouse carryall. The driver flicked his horse with the reins. Mrs. Fox, in a panic, stood up and called to Dorrie in her high, cracked voice.

"Don't forget, dear. I'll be expecting to hear. Don't forget."

"I'll not forget," Dorrie promised, her throat aching. Poor, poor old people.

Mrs. Fox sat down, her hands folded stiffly, her bonnet ribbons streaming gallantly in the breeze as the wagon drove on.

"A plucky girl, Belle Fox," Jule said, her eyes suddenly old and bewildered. "I remember her wedding."

"What makes you think you're going to bring her here to Grandma's?" Linda asked Dorrie challengingly.

"Now—now—" Jule remonstrated.

"Never mind," Dorrie was defiant. "I'm going to look after her and I don't need your help, Linda Shirley, I thank you."

Her eyes, like Jule's, were suddenly old and bewildered.

Chapter Eight

May drifted lazily into June. The attic bedroom was very still for many days. Old books lay neglected at the foot of the bed or sliding down sprawled open on the floor. On the night table stood a glass of stale water, and a spider had spanned it. Dust drifted through the air, and the rats had been encouraged by silence to gnaw a passage through from the attic.

Propped up on his wrinkled yellow pillows, his soiled sheets dragging on the floor, old Wickley stared into space from morning until night. He did not so much as open one of his books. He dreamed old men's dreams and sometimes his lips moved in a whisper.

The letters no longer came from Roger. Dorrie and Jule were worried.

"Maybe he's dead," Jule said thoughtfully. "I remember hearing him say he was in New York now. It's a dangerous place."

Dorrie cried a little, then. She had built such a beautiful image of Roger III. She had held long conversations with this divinity for years.

"Mr. Wickley," she asked timidly one day, "Roger all right? I mean your grandson in the East."

The old man's shaggy brows drew together in an effort at concentration. His skin had dried up and hung in sagging tucks on his cheekbones.

"Roger? Roger?" He drew long fingers shakily across his eyes. "I don't know, child. Roger? Oh, yes. The little boy, Roger. Perhaps he will come here for a little while with me. We are all each other has."

He drew a long breath.

"Alone such a long time," he whimpered. "Sixty years . . . She . . . she went away on our first anniversary . . . with the baby. That was my own Roger . . . I only saw him twice . . . then after he grew up . . . He died. I wonder if the little Roger is like him. Perhaps he will come. Perhaps."

Dorrie was happy again. Her adored hero had not been killed after all. She could go on dreaming about him. And someday when she was tall and beautiful like Linda, he would come to Birchfield and fall madly in love with her.

"Only I'm past seventeen," she reflected. "And if I'm ever going to be tall and beautiful, I'd better begin right now."

Mr. Wickley's eyes closed wearily. He was very tired, but he must not die until he'd seen the boy. Sometimes his lids would drag over his eyes and he would catch a dim quivering outline of a girl's head. Slanting golden eyes peered at him through the troublesome fog, and he had to blink sharply to be sure they were Dorrie's eyes and not those great yellow velvet-legged spiders that sometimes crawled in from the apple tree outside his window.

The shelves of ancient books pressed on him. They closed in on him like ghouls about a coffin. His eyes filmed, remembering that philosophers were ghouls, feeding on death. But he had loved them so. It was not fair that they should gloat on his passing.

Golden spider-legged eyes compelled him to life again. When they vanished, he would go, too . . . the books would gently smother him. *Esse est percipi* . . . He would be a shred of parchment on the pillow.

"Mr. Wickley—Mr. Wickley—"

Two topazes caught in black lace . . . A girl's eyes. And now he caught the cloud of brown hair above and a shadowy face . . . Dorrie . . .

"I asked you when Roger is coming. Do you think he will come to my commencement, Mr. Wickley?"

His eyelids were stiff and tired. He didn't want to open them again. He had lived too long . . . that much he knew. Eighty years too long . . . His lids lifted painfully. He must know if those eyes were still there. Two balls of dull gold—staring, unwinking, terrible . . . idol's eyes! . . . Fear hurtled through his body and gripped his heart. His body jerked forward and his glazing eyes hunted desperately through the fog for those other golden eyes. Ah, blindfolded, with his poor arms nailed to his sides . . . A wind blew through the room.

Dorrie sat on the window seat, looking out over the birches. Young Roger would come across that path and he would be very young and strong and marvelously handsome. He would look up toward the attic window and when he saw her waiting there for him, he would come straight to her.

"When Roger comes, Mr. Wickley," she began. "When Roger comes—"

She turned toward the old man, and bewilderment crept over her face. His mouth had dropped open as if in wonder at the ancient incredible vision before his wide staring eyes. A yellow waxen hand dangled over the bedside. Dorrie stood frozen, terrified. Flies buzzed through the window. A bold rat thrust his snout through the hole in the floor and then scampered back to his nest. A book clattered to the floor.

Dorrie drew a long, quivering breath and fled madly down the stairs. Roger came.

Dorrie was sitting up in her own attic window when he arrived at Jule's. She had been looking through old trunks in hope of finding material for a commencement dress. Grandmother said there might be some white satin and lace from her mother's wedding dress. No one had heart for Dorrie's commencement preparations while the undertaker's chairs lay piled on the porch, dreary reminders of an old man's shabby funeral.

Dorrie thrust exploring fingers down into the disheveled mystery of the bottom layer. The stillness of the adjoining room echoed somberly through her heart. Dorrie wiped her eyes on a scrap of plaid taffeta. Poor old Mr. Wickley.

She and Grandmother were the only ones who had cried at the funeral.

"It wasn't any surprise to him," Ella Morris unfeelingly said. "Old folks expect to die."

"Dirty old man," Linda had said, sulkily scrubbing the floor of his bedroom. "It's about time something happened to give me a chance at this room. How any human being can live in such filth!"

It was Linda who had written to Roger III. There had been a New York address on the letter that came the day the old man died.

"Somebody's got to come and take his junk away," she declared resolutely to the moist-eyed Jule. "His grandson was coming anyway, so it won't hurt him to take charge of his affairs. Who paid for his funeral?"

Jule pretended to be too absorbed in sorrow to hear, but Dorrie defended her.

"Never you mind, Linda Shirley," she said, a catch in her voice. "I guess Grandma can do what she pleases for an old friend."

Leaning against the trunk, Dorrie cried a little. She didn't mind his dying so much, but it hurt to see how cruel people could be about other people. She smoothed out the plaid silk and traced the pattern with her fingers. Then she reached down into the trunk again. She found the creamy lace and satin that had been her mother's bridal gown in the very bottom and pulled it over to the little window.

"It's beautiful," she breathed, holding it against her cheek. She sat cross-legged, leaning back on the trunk, the shining fabric trailing across her lap. She was wishing she could wear it as it was, train and all.

The attic door creaked on its hinges and flew open. Dorrie hadn't heard the step on the stairs, so she looked up, startled . . . He stood in the doorway, his hand on the knob. And he was very tall and straight and his mouth was stern and resolute.

He was more inaccessibly handsome than Dorrie had ever dreamed, with a lean muscular grace and strong, highbred features. His black hair swept back from his high forehead, and his brows were a straight, uncompromising line.

Dorrie's heart fluttered.

"You're Roger," she stammered. She ached with disappointment, for this distinguished, stern-eyed man would never notice a pale young girl who didn't even look the eighteen years she claimed. If there had only been a crinkle about his eyes to show that he had smiled once, or if there were only a droop to his mouth to show he had once felt sorry for something!

He didn't look the least bit like Birchfield. The way his gray tweed suit set about his shoulders, even the slant of his collar and the twist of his tie, reminded Dorrie vaguely of those mysterious young men who leaned idly out of dining car windows or smoked cigarettes on the back platforms of Pullmans on the New York trains.

"Is this the room my grandfather had?" he asked.

His voice was low and tired, and Dorrie suspected that he had been ill. She brightened, for somewhere in the voice was a fugitive tenderness.

"This is just the attic," she hurried to explain. "Mr. Wickley's room is next door. Let me show you."

"By no means," he motioned her to sit still. "I would not think of destroying such a charming picture. I will find the room. Thank you."

Dorrie stared after him as he withdrew. He thought she made a charming picture! But he hadn't really looked at her, had he? She dropped the lace on the floor and tiptoed out, almost without volition, so magnetized was she by this strange young man. He had entered the old bedroom, and Dorrie slid in after him.

"These are the ones he liked best," she said eagerly, motioning to the books on the table. "I knew you'd want to know which were his favorites so I collected them for you."

Roger's fingers leafed the volumes on the table with a loving, practiced air. An exclamation escaped his lips.

"Oh, I say, this is too bad! We could have got on so beautifully."

"Yes, isn't it too bad?" Dorrie agreed. "You like the same books he did, don't you?"

"Apparently." Roger ran through a worn volume of Jowett's *Plato*. He seemed to take Dorrie's presence for granted. She stood by the window, her hands clasped behind her green gingham dress. She could not take her eyes away from young Roger.

"He'll fall in love with Linda," she thought, "And Linda will be horrid to him. Oh, I can't bear to see her humiliate him. She will, though, if he falls in love with her. Even if I didn't love him, I'd be kind to him because he is so proud . . . But Linda's different."

"Did you know my grandfather well?" he asked, directing his gray eyes toward Dorrie.

"He was my best friend," Dorrie explained . . . Realities were so different from dreams, except that Roger was more wonderful than she had been able to imagine—hard and cold and beautiful. Ice.

"You know this place—your grandmother and the house and all," Roger waved his arm in a comprehensive gesture. "It's wonderful. I had no idea it would be like this. If I'd known grandfather lived in such a place, I would have come to see him long ago. It's priceless, really."

Dorrie was a little uncertain as to what he meant. He couldn't think the house was beautiful because it was really terribly old. Yesterday part of the ceiling in Esther Mason's bedroom fell down.

"There's always a lot of excitement," she confessed. "And Grandmother and I like that. There was a snake charmer here a little while ago."

"No!" The smile that flickered in Roger's eyes was a dazzling thing. No, he couldn't be ice after all. Perhaps that was his protection and underneath he might be warm.

"And lots of actresses," Dorrie went on.

Roger's eyes rested a little curiously on Dorrie's eager face. "What's your name?"

"Dorrie," she replied. "Theodora Shirley is my whole name. But I don't like Theodora, do you?"

"Rather pompous for you," the young man agreed. "I should have called you Anne—or perhaps Primrose."

Dorrie pondered this and a slight smile hovered over the man's lips.

"But Dorrie will do," he assured her. "It's a soft, gentle name—and still a little fond of dolls."

"But I'm not that sort of person," Dorrie protested, getting a little pink.

Roger looked up in surprise.

"What sort of person are you, then?" he inquired. Dorrie hesitated.

"I—I guess I don't know," she was obliged to admit.

They studied each other frankly for a brief while. Roger saw a white-faced girl of seventeen or more, slight, grave-eyed, with a charming, gusty voice.

Dorrie saw her divinity.

* * *

Everyone had to go to the reception the night before commencement. There were speeches and punch and dancing. Dorrie had, with Jule's help, made up the old wedding dress into a lovely gown—at least it was lovely to Dorrie's tolerant eyes. At Ella Morris's suggestion a large silk sash was added to give a modish touch.

"Will Phil bring you home?" Linda asked as she helped Dorrie to dress that night. "And what wrap are you going to wear?"

Dorrie squirmed a little uneasily. She had not anticipated Linda's sisterly aid in her toilet, and had in fact thought Linda was going to the movies with Marie Farley—an excellent opportunity to appropriate Linda's own best coat.

"Grandma says I can wear her white shawl," she said.

Linda's lips tightened. She didn't want her sister to go out in that old-fashioned "fascinator," but if she let her wear her own coat, it would assuredly be ruined. Dorrie was always spilling things if she wasn't tearing them on rusty nails. Linda decided to let well enough alone. No one would notice the shawl anyway.

"I do hope you don't have to come all the way home alone," she said. "All through the North End and down Main Street. That trip from the school gym isn't nice late at night."

Dorrie was too preoccupied with her own mirrored charms to be worried as to how she was going to get home. The lace was so soft and lovely. It hung over the old satin in tiers of flounces and there was a bertha over her sloping white shoulders. Linda commented on the holes in the lace, but these were things that Dorrie's eyes seldom dwelt upon.

She hoped Roger Wickley would see her. He had only seen her in ginghams that made her look like a perfect infant. But in a long, ruffled party dress with her nose powdered, she looked almost as old as Linda.

She thought she would go out the side door so that if he were in his room with the door open, he would see her.

"Now for heaven's sake, don't let Mr. Wickley see you," exhorted Linda, pinning up a torn ruffle. "Better go out the back way. I'd hate to have him see you in that old-fashioned thing because he's used to New York girls and their evening dresses. He'd probably think we were terribly behind the times to wear a dress like this."

Dorrie's face fell. She had thought she looked so well! It alarmed her a little that Linda should care what Roger thought. It wasn't like Linda to respect any of her grandmother's people. Maybe—oh, dear—maybe she was falling in love with Roger!

But Roger saw her leaving in spite of Linda. He was just coming in from a walk and stood looking at Dorrie with some concern.

"See here," he said. "Is it quite the thing for you to be going alone to this affair? Isn't it a fairish distance?"

"I'm not afraid," Dorrie told him, smiling radiantly at his thoughtfulness. "Besides it isn't dark yet."

"And some young man will of course see you home when it does get dark," Roger said with an amused shrug. Dorrie saw him looking after her as she walked toward the gate, and her heart beat very fast.

Mrs. Miller, Mrs. Remer, and Mrs. Riggs, the mayor's wife, were the official chaperones of the party, but of course all the high school teachers were there, too. They stood in a little group near the orchestra platform and shook hands with everyone. The four young teachers wore evening dresses left over from their not so remote college proms, and each hoped fervently that the young assistant principal would single her out for special attention. After the music started—Miss Lundquist and Chester Riggs formed the orchestra for the evening—they sat down in little separate corners with the younger people, and the teachers beamed with bright tranquility as if they loved to see the young folks enjoy themselves. And they sent sly, demure glances toward the assistant principal.

Miss Carl, the pretty blonde English teacher, acting on a charitable impulse, sat down beside Dorrie. The child seemed so forlorn on these school affairs. Always the wrong clothes, and tonight she wore a long, glittering necklace which very clearly had come from the ten-cent store. It was too bad, really, for the girl was genuinely talented . . . Miss Carl felt that she was doing the big thing in sitting down beside this unfortunate youngster. She even condescended to engage her in conversation.

"Such a sweet party," she said with a friendly, but of course not too friendly, smile. "I hope you are having a nice time, Theodora."

"Oh, yes," said Theodora casually. Miss Carl was so pretty. Dorrie watched her covertly. But her hair wasn't as pretty as Linda's.

The teacher fanned herself benignly while the young assistant principal fox-trotted zestfully by with Miss Truet.

"Such pretty dresses, too," she commented. "Doesn't our little Molly look adorable?"

Little Molly was dancing with one thin arm tightly around Phil Lancer's blushing neck. Dorrie made an inarticulate reply.

"You don't dance?" politely queried Miss Carl.

"Yes," said Dorrie in some confusion. "I haven't been asked yet."

"Perhaps Walter will ask you," encouraged Miss Carl.

Walter was the fat boy. He danced with whatever girl had no excuse to offer. Dorrie was not heartened at the prospect of Walter. But it was nice of Miss Carl to speak to her. Perhaps she would ask her about her future. You usually spoke to teachers about futures at commencement time. But would she dare tell her about the brown ledger?

"Miss Carl, I wonder—" she began shyly, fingering the lovely string of beads Mrs. Winslow had given to her. "I wonder if I could show you some of my poems sometime?"

"Poems?" Miss Carl's eyebrows lifted. "How interesting, Theodora!"

"You see, no one's ever seen them," Dorrie explained. "But now that it's time to choose a profession I thought—if you said they were good enough—I'd become a poet."

Miss Carl smiled and plucked her fan thoughtfully.

"Well, my dear child, as for making poetry a profession—"

She stopped there, for Mrs. Eph Miller, magnificent in a genuine black velvet evening dress, was coming toward her, electing a hazardous route directly across the middle of the dance floor with couples all about her bouncing up and down in Birchfield's own version of the Boston. Mrs. Eph Miller was on the school board. Mrs. Eph Miller was president of the Browning Club. Mrs. Eph Miller kept two servants.

"Why, how are you, Mrs. Miller?" breathed the flattered Miss Carl, extending an eager hand.

There was room on the bench for three people, but Mrs. Miller stood up. She spoke to Miss Carl, but her eye was on Dorrie. Dorrie wriggled under that eye.

"I wanted to have a chat with you before you went away for the summer," said the grand lady.

"Of course," hastily murmured Miss Carl, her face flushed at this unexpected honor. "Do sit down—"

Then she remembered the Shirley girl beside her, and that false jewelry. She looked at her with polite inquiry, as if she had only this moment realized who this person was. Gracious! She did hope Mrs. Miller wouldn't think she approved of the girl, or indeed had the remotest interest in those awful Shirleys.

"Why, yes—I'll sit down," Mrs. Miller said, staring coldly at Dorrie.

"Oh!" Dorrie exclaimed, getting to her feet. "You wanted this seat—"

Mrs. Miller sat down and Miss Carl promptly turned her back on Dorrie. Dorrie stood for a moment, embarrassed. She was the only person standing up in the whole hall, except the dancers. She was conscious of Miss Carl's open slight. She was aware of several eyes upon her.

"A lot I care," she thought indignantly. "They don't trouble me at all."

But she sat down farther off a little weakly. In that moment it came over her that her dress was horrid—simply horrid. The lace was old and torn and out of date. Everyone else had on stiff taffeta dresses in beautiful pastel shades . . . And no one else wore a sash. Hers stuck out in two big wings at the back. And the lovely glittering necklace which she had cherished for months—it burned her throat. It was wrong—terribly, frightfully wrong. She almost ran to the dressing room in her haste to take it off.

No one was in the dressing room. She sat down with a little sigh of relief. If she only dared go home. But if she went now, they would all know she wasn't having a good time, and probably they'd laugh. And if she got home so early, Roger would think she hadn't been the belle of the ball after all . . .

She stayed in the dingy little room for centuries, it seemed. When girls came in to powder their noses between dances, she hastily began fumbling with her slipper, as if it were hurting too much for her to dance. Miss Carl came in once and didn't glance at her. After a while Dorrie went back to the dance floor and sat on the edge of a chair near the door. Now people were beginning to go home . . . She would wait five more minutes and go, for it wouldn't be conspicuous, then.

She saw Phil Lancer looking at her at the beginning of the dance. Molly Miller was dancing with Carl Hodge, and Phil had no partner. He looked quickly away as Dorrie's eyes met his . . . It was the home waltz. Dorrie ran thankfully down to the dressing room again. Molly Miller and the girls were there, changing their pumps and powdering. Molly was reaching up for her evening cape.

"What is this awful thing?" she exclaimed, taking a wrap down gingerly in two fingers and dropping it. "Right on top of my perfectly good new cape."

"My *dear*!" cried Lucy Remer, picking up the offending garment and extending it at arm's length. "Look! Where on earth did it come from!"

"Good heavens!" gurgled Molly. "It's an old-time fascinator."

"Probably the janitress left it here when she was cleaning," someone said. "Isn't it a perfect scream?"

"Maybe—" Molly Miller said, struck with a thought. "Oh, girls—maybe—sh! There she is!"

Dorrie glanced unseeingly at her image in the mirror, and walked out, her grandmother's shawl left lying in a heap on the floor. She walked jauntily across the floor and down to the street, oblivious to the crowd surging along with her homeward. Couples followed her, passed her, as she made her solitary way down North Street. Never had a street seemed so long. Other girls whispered to their beaus as they passed her. . . Dorrie held her head very high and walked very sedately, her butterfly sash standing out behind her, her uncovered party dress oddly out of place on the dingy side street.

She turned down the main street. More couples passed her, whispering, tittering. She passed the poolroom and heard someone whistle insolently after her. She breathed a little harder. She didn't care! She didn't care! She didn't care!

She came to Elm Street and turned the corner. No one else lived that way. She could run now if she wanted to. But perhaps some eyes might still be peering at her, twinkling gleefully because she was unhappy. No, she could not run.

Dorrie held her head very stiffly and walked carefully with measured steps, down Elm Street across the railroad tracks, past the birches—as if she were marching to music. Her party dress, white and foamy under the midnight moon, burned into her flesh. The birches swayed with laughter and mocking whispers.

She marched across the lawn, numbly, her lips set. She was not Dorrie Shirley now, but a mechanical doll with a hard, knobby thing for a heart and a whirring thing for a brain. Someone moaned when she reached the steps—a very tiny moan. Dorrie realized with a shock that it must have escaped from her own lips!

Roger was standing against the porch pillar, smoking a cigarette. At the slight cry he stepped forward involuntarily, the cigarette dropping from his fingers.

"Why, child—dear child—" she heard him say in a voice more gently, heartbreakingly sympathetic than anything she had ever known. "What is it?"

She walked across the cobblestone path—straight into the arms of the only kind person in the world.

Chapter Nine

There was something fiercely protective in Roger's feeling for Dorrie after the reception night. She had sobbed vehemently in his arms for a few minutes and then abruptly brushed her arm across her face and ran into the house. He could understand far more than what her broken sentences had told him and it made him angry at the whole world.

"Abominable!" he muttered, stalking about his room savagely. "A sensitive little thing like that. They're setting out to crush her and it's not fair. By God, they shan't."

The medieval knight in him arose to the challenge of a frail woman in peril. Dorrie was no longer merely an interesting child to him but a cloudy ideal to be protected by his hard masculine strength from the dangers that crowded about her.

"Danger!" reflected Roger, surprised that this thought had not struck him the instant of his arrival in this strange house. "Why, the girl is in all sorts of danger. That old crippled, vulture, and that cheap little streetwalker are poisonous for an artistic type like Dorrie. And that beautiful icebound sister could tramp all over Dorrie's poor little self. How can the girl stand up to all of it with this wretched little town cracking the whip all the time? How could anyone stand up to it alone?"

So Roger set out to rescue his lady. He smiled a little ironically, obsessed as he now was with the desire to help Dorrie, when he recalled that he had looked forward to this brief absence from New York as an opportunity to consider his own career with detachment and to build new fortresses in his mind against the perils of the future. He had gotten a little confused this last year. He himself was so self-sufficient, taught to be so by his solitary school camp and foreign hotel upbringing. Since emerging from college, he had steeled himself to be even more independent of the world that he might write what was in him to write untouched by concern for other men's standards or human demands. How easy it would be for him to be swept into this new war, to join the French army as a few of his romantic classmates had already done! How simple and yet how weak. He gloried in the analytical mind that could always save him from his emotions. He was certain that complete self-sufficiency was the thing a writer must have at the very outset. He wished he could teach Dorrie Shirley this virtue so that she might go on unhurt by the creeping evil about her.

One day they sat in old Wickley's disordered room, sorting out the books, and Roger found himself telling Dorrie things that he had never spoken of to a living soul, in his desire to teach her the secret of self-sufficiency. About his own writing . . . the whole plan for his trilogy. She sat on the window seat, clasping her hands intensely, her eyes wide with excitement. Oh, he could teach her many things, Roger thought—strength enough to carry herself remote from taints after he had gone back to New York.

"For years," he told her earnestly, "I have had only one desire—to get an attic somewhere and write—write at any cost. I will never be crushed by a system—domestic or economic—that much I vowed. I am going to write my novels and nothing—nothing is to get in my way. Work will be my armor against pain."

"But how can you shut everything out?" Dorrie asked.

Roger thrust his hand through his black hair and began to pace the room.

"Because I have learned to be ruthless, as you must learn to be if you're not to be hurt by life," he answered. "It's the only way anyone can live. I've seen too many artists compromise with themselves not to know that weakness is destruction. Oh, I've seen! Why, Dorrie, I have denied myself everything that might give me pleasure—and I could be a sybarite, I assure you, if I chose—when it took me from the work I had set for myself. Women—"

"Women?" Dorrie repeated blankly. Roger waved his hand impatiently.

"Naturally—and above all—women. They crowd everything else out if you admit them. And as for marriage, it's out of the question for a sincere writer. You have to choose between being an artist and cad, or being a hack and gentleman. If I could let my wife starve while I did my ideal work, then I'd be an artist, but I'd also be a cad. If I wrote tenth-rate trash for money to keep a family decently, then I'd be a gentleman but I'd also be a hack. Oh, I hate these compromises . . . The only way to avoid them is to shut out women and direct your passions toward creative work."

He stood looking absently into space, his dark brows lowering over his moody eyes. He had forgotten Dorrie. She was in the trance his conversation always threw her. She studied him speculatively, troubled by that steel in him, until he whirled about and gave her a funny twisted smile.

"You're wondering why I say these absurd things to you," he said. "Well—I wonder, too. I suppose it's advice—advice to both of us. Anyway, I want you to have your own world where these people can't touch you."

Her own world . . . Dorrie thought of the garret. Roger was the one person she might admit to her world.

He followed her a little wonderingly into the garret and sat down on the creaky floor near the old portraits and broken old trunks. A little puzzled, he took the old brown ledger Dorrie put into his hands.

"I wanted you to see," she said. "You see—this—well, this is *me*."

Roger's lean strong face was disturbingly enigmatical. It revealed no emotion to Dorrie's watchful eyes. Did he like her poetry? Because if he didn't she would burn it at once. Here was her own true self, and if Roger did not understand, she would be unhappy always. She looked away from him as he read to brace herself for his criticism. Her lips felt dry and white . . . Perhaps he would not know, but it was her very heart she was offering to his eyes.

Roger's hard brown fingers leafed page after page. The lines about the attic in starlight . . . About Claire . . . Now he put his hand over his gray absorbed eyes to study a difficult phrase . . . Hill sonnets . . . Things about people . . . Towns in darkness . . . Queer little verses about insects and tiny things from her eightyear-old imaginings . . . Formal twelve-year-old reflections on love . . . Shy, adolescent yearnings for remote things, intimations of passion . . .

"Perhaps," Dorrie said, carefully, looking out the window, "I shouldn't have shown them to you . . . If you don't mind, Roger, I'd rather you didn't say anything just now. You see, I—I—"

Roger closed the book and looked at her from beneath somber, black brows for a long time without speaking. When he did speak, his voice had a curious, hushed quality that made Dorrie's amber eyes widen unbelievingly.

"My dear," he said, "You are a poet—a real poet. I would give my soul to express the beauty in me as marvelously as you have expressed the beauty that is in you, Dorrie Shirley."

Dorrie's hands tightened, and her eyes closed. The thing that was in her—that dark pool—was beautiful to Roger . . .

Roger Wickley stared in silence out the window. A slight smile, an ironic thing, tugged at his mouth. He was going to protect this girl from the world about her! When the only world she had ever known was the enchanted lovely world of her own fancy!

Protect her? Did he not, rather, need to envy her?

Linda was very silent about Roger. He puzzled her. Plainly he was a gentleman. But on the other hand, his grandfather had been half-crazy. His polite cold reserve pleased her. Yet she had heard him discussing the most ridiculous things with Dorrie. Worse, she had seen Dorrie using Esther Mason's rouge, and Roger had treated the young painted girl with even more deference than he treated Linda herself.

"He's grateful to Dorrie because she was nice to the old gentleman," Jule explained. "I'm sure it's very kind of him."

"But, Grandmother," said Linda sharply, "I do wish she wouldn't paint. You used to laugh when she was little and daubed herself up, but Dorrie's nearly eighteen now, and when girls that old paint, people think it means something."

"Like as not Dorrie'll be another Esther Mason," placidly observed Ella Morris. "I shouldn't be at all surprised. She's that excitable nature."

"If she does the things Esther Mason does I'll not have her for a sister," Linda said, her eyes flashing angrily at the invalid. "How dare you say such a thing?"

Ella's calm remained unruffled.

"Young Roger thinks she's all right, I notice," she said, and then a new thought struck her. "Maybe you saw Gertrude Stall stopping in my room on her way to her lesson today."

"I believe I did," Linda admitted, affecting nonchalance. "Why?"

Ella emitted a chuckle.

"Know what she wanted? Wanted to know if I'd mind introducing her to the new roomer because she wanted him for her party next week."

"I introduced her all right," continued Ella, with her usual enjoyment of another's discomfiture even when it was a Stall's, "and he gave her that cold, faraway look of his—he's his granddad all over, you know—and the poor girl was too scared to ask him. I felt real sorry for her . . . But you know young Mr. Wickley's a real handsome young man. You don't see them like that in this town."

"Wasn't it a pity," said Jule, "that he didn't take to Gertrude when he might have had such a nice time at her party? It must be lonely out here for a young New York fellow with nobody to talk to. Why, I don't believe he's talked to anybody but Dorrie."

"No," said Linda. If the new roomer were as conspicuous as all that, then she'd certainly have to scold Dorrie good for getting herself up so when she went walking with him.

"Wonder what he thinks of this place," she pondered aloud.

"Not much, I guess," Ella tittered. "He started out for an early walk, oh, it must have been before five this morning, and ran plunk into Esther just coming in. Been out all night with some fellow, you could tell. I was taking my medicine and happened to look out the window. Guess he can tell pretty much about the place now."

Linda drew her mouth in disgustedly. There it was again. The same old story.

Jule glanced at the clock. It was almost six.

"I wish Dorrie'd come in," she frowned. "I declare that girl hasn't been a bit of use ever since young Wickley came."

"Was she in for lunch?" asked Ella slyly.

"Why, no," Jule said after a moment's thought.

"They went past my window about noon," Ella divulged, veiling the sparkle in her eye. "Doesn't seem to me that's the way to pack books."

* * *

They came in together not long afterward, and something about their silence made Jule knit her gray brows thoughtfully. Silence—that wasn't like Dorrie. Her face was flushed, too, and her eyes shone. Jule looked cautiously at Linda to see if the older girl read anything in this extraordinary state. But Linda's mind was on something else, and as soon as Roger had gone to his room, she expressed it.

"You ought to be ashamed, Dorrie Shirley," she whispered. "Painting your face and wearing a silk dress for a walk in the country. Mr. Wickley must be perfectly disgusted. I'm sure he's ashamed to be seen with you."

Instead of her usual airy dismissal of reproaches, Dorrie listened attentively. She rubbed her cheeks.

"Maybe it would be better not to rouge," she said meekly. "I just like to, that's all. I wasn't thinking of whether he liked it or not. We talk about so many other things. But maybe he'd rather I didn't paint."

Linda was so puzzled by this new Dorrie that she did not pursue the subject, and Dorrie went up to her attic to sit alone in the dusk. Up there she took the pins out of her bronze hair. Then she knelt by the little window now framing two stars and a new moon, and with her head drooping back and eyes closed, she set for herself the exquisite task of remembering every word that Roger had said to her that day.

Between the oak and the Carver's barn he had said, "I want to know how you feel about Kenman. Does he seem as interesting to you as my island characters?"

And again—

"You're the only person in the whole world with whom I've dared talk over my things before they're done. Everyone else says exactly the thing to kill them before I've even borne them."

Between the barn and the old bridge he had said, "You'll understand what I mean when you come to New York, Dorrie."

At the bend in the Birchfield road, he had said, "Look at that sky, my dear!"

He had helped her over the Whateley's fence. Which hand had he touched? Dorrie tried to recall, but then there was no need. It was her left one that still tingled.

At the cider mill he had said, "By the way, Dorrie, how old are you? About fifteen or is it a hundred?"

"Twenty," she had said, modestly, and it almost seemed true. He had looked at her a little quizzically.

"I mean right now?" he had added, and Dorrie had the grace to blush.

"About eighteen," she confessed.

"You women!" he had said then.

What was it he had said at Elm Tree Corners? Dorrie was in a panic lest one precious phrase had escaped her. Oh, yes—

"You're just the person to find in that house. Linda's all wrong. When I write about it, I'll leave her out."

"Don't you like Linda?" Dorrie had asked.

Roger shrugged.

"I'm a mere novelist, not a poet," he had replied. "I'm more interested in beating hearts than in sonnets in marble."

At the old Taylor homestead he had said—

"Do you know, I'm going to think a great deal of this Birchfield of yours, Dorrie? And do you mind if I write to you? You help clear up things amazingly for me."

Then all the way home they had not exchanged one word, but at the bridge he had suddenly smiled down at her. And at the gate he had touched her arm. And in the kitchen he had looked at her all the time he was talking to Grandmother.

Dorrie opened her eyes and breathed a deep, warm sigh. She was aware of someone in Mr. Wickley's room—Roger, of course. At each sound her heart leaped. Once he came so close to the thin partitions that she could hear him breathe. A little gasp escaped her at such thrilling intimacy.

But mostly her feeling for Roger, as she leaned from her attic window, was pain—a strange, unbearable lovely pain.

And Dorrie knew that this was love.

* * *

Of one thing Roger Wickley had always been sure, marriage was not for him.

With a clear, straight-seeing eye he had seen only peril in such an adventure, peril for his soul. To the gigantic career he had set for himself women could be merely a decorative fringe, a graceful interlude. True, there were times when he thought of a slim cool gracious woman who might in later, more luxurious years become Mrs. Roger Wickley. A woman of discreet charm, with more breeding than cleverness . . . A smooth costly woman who received passion with a cool pliant tolerance but preferred an epigram. Such a woman would receive his adoration and keep herself ever aloof. He would be lonely and sometimes desperately unhappy, but out of loneliness grew his most profound ideas, and unhappiness induced him to an inconceivable amount of work.

A marriage with this nebulous creature would be ideal, for such a woman would permit him to remain a distinct individual, leaving his fire for creation rather than wasting it in feverish desires. This dim ideal lay in the back of Roger's mind. But Birchfield had fretted his whole soul with queer unexpected tangles.

For here was a white-faced girl with honey-colored eyes, with a small drooping scarlet mouth and swirling bronze hair . . . a mere child for all her eighteen years, and Roger was obsessed with her. He was enchanted by her, eager for her voice, the shy grave upward glance. Her charm was that of a foreign woman for him; she knew so amusingly little of this world, living as she had in a hidden empire all her life. Sometimes he forgot she was young and talked of himself as he would never have talked to the proud lady of his dreams. She would make oddly wise comments and listen with an eager sympathy that startled him because it weakened him. He, who had meant to be always self-sufficient, beginning to lean on understanding. He, who had armored himself against all women—enchanting, luscious Viennese women, brittle fascinating Parisiennes, softthroated, coal-eyed Spanish girls—he, who had said that henceforth all passion must go into his art—suddenly, unreasonably, ridiculously caught by a breathless voice, a little rushing laugh, and two haunting golden eyes.

"Lucky for my peace of mind I'm leaving in a few days," he reflected, irritated at himself. "Probably the whole thing is a mental sympathy—something I've never had with a woman—something that can go on indefinitely in correspondence. That's exactly what it is. Lucky, too, that I've had enough experience not to want to make this a physical thing."

Dorrie lay awake all night remembering every word he had said each day. Sometimes at daybreak she slipped out of bed and sat by the window, watching the dawn and thinking of Roger. Sometimes her heart choked her so that she could scarcely breathe. When she heard his footsteps, her veins throbbed and beat in her temples and throat and clenched hands.

"I can't bear it till he goes away," Dorrie thought once, "I can't live all hot and cold like this, day and night, forever. When he goes away, perhaps, I can cry. That would help."

When he smiled down at her from his great height, and his dark eyes crinkled slowly at the corners, Dorrie wanted to weep. He was so remote, so inaccessible because of his stern perfection. Oh, she was not beautiful like Linda, and she was not clever like women in books, so there couldn't be so much he could see in her. But she could write poetry and she would write such glorious immortal things that he would have to admire her, even if he couldn't love her. And he had told her of his own accord that he would rather be with her than anyone else.

She went about the house in a trance. Jule, a sentimentalist herself, was vaguely irritated by the same quality in others and scolded her younger grandchild occasionally for absent-mindedness. Later, her concern over Lew Mason's desolate plight, and her desire to keep from Linda the news of Esther's fortnightly absence, crowded Dorrie's matter out of her thoughts. But Linda was not wholly blind. She called Dorrie into her room one night.

"You don't leave poor Mr. Wickley alone one minute, Dorrie," she accused. "I'm sure he must get terribly bored with a young girl hanging around him all the time, only he's too polite to say so. He's nice to you because he thinks you helped take care of the old man, but good heavens, Dorrie, you're too old to be trailing after him the way you do."

Dorrie said nothing. She hadn't heard a word Linda said. She was thinking that in another day or two Roger would be gone, and she would be unhappy forever. So she only looked at her sister and answered vaguely.

"And I wish you wouldn't wear that old silk again on the streets," Linda concluded. She jerked a box from the depths of her closet—the box containing her yellow organdy. "Here's this old thing you can have if you go out again. I hate it. Tell Grandma to take up the hem for you."

Dorrie's eyes glowed at the prospect of a pretty frock to wear for Roger's last night. She thanked Linda and hurried down the stairs.

Roger had everything packed next day and took his bags over to stay at the Birchfield House that night so that the lady acrobats from the Star might have his room. The blonde lady acrobat had written Aunt Jule in advance for the room and was disposed to be very touchy on finding it occupied, in spite of Aunt Jule's assurance that Mr. Wickley would be out in ten minutes.

"I'm ready to drop," Judy declared resentfully, pulling off her hat and tossing it on Jule's piano. "I want to go to bed this minute. Not in ten minutes. This very minute."

But when the door opened and the darkly handsome young man in well-cut tweeds appeared, Judy's jaw dropped. *She* didn't want to put Mr. Wickley out. Not for worlds. Her eye dwelt hungrily on his broad shoulders, the slant of his jaw. No, she wouldn't dream of putting Mr. Wickley out on her account. She could just sleep on the cot here in the living room. As a special favor, wouldn't Mr. Wickley please keep the room tonight?

But the gray-eyed young man merely smiled, bowed, and went on out.

"Ho hum," jeered Judy's slight swarthy companion. "Look what he turned you down for."

Judy saw a slight figure in a light dress walking down to the gate with the young man.

"Mon Dew," she ejaculated. "The landlady's granddaughter. Say it ain't so, Birdie, say it ain't so."

"That's her," jibed the other. "Don't spoil their act, Judy, just for the sake of an evening's thrill. Fat chance you'd have, anyway, with these rustic flappers . . . Snap out of it, dearie, and help me out of this damned dress."

* * *

They walked along the river road that night, and then back to Jule's front porch. Strangely enough Roger could find little to talk of, and was annoyed at the queer discontent that had come over him at the prospect of going back to New York. Dorrie was silent, but it was a breathlessly happy silence. Roger's lean muscular fingers gripped her arm—how tightly neither of them realized until Dorrie found the bruises the next day.

"It's done me good to get away from my writing for a while," he said as they returned to the house. "I was getting too tied up in it. Losing perspective and all."

Dorrie settled herself and her airy flounces on the top step of the porch, Roger lounging on the step beneath.

"You ought to get away every few months," she said sagely. She wanted to add, "and come to Birchfield," but that would never do.

Roger gave a short laugh. He flung away his cigarette.

"All I can do to stay put in New York, let alone raise funds to get away," he said drily. "My income from my mother's estate is exactly seventy-five dollars a month. I shall live on crackers and cheese for weeks to make up for this trip."

Seventy-five dollars seemed a great deal to Dorrie. She couldn't remember ever having had more than two dollars at once. That could buy most anything . . . She leaned her chin on her hands and looked up at the dim moon.

"But won't you be very rich when you sell your first novel?" she asked hopefully. "It will be done soon, won't it?"

"I know," Roger nodded. "But even if I do sell it—and mind you, I intend that it shall sell—it isn't the kind of thing that brings in money. You'll see when you read it . . . No, Dorrie, my dear, I fear the next two or three years will have to be spent in a very bare studio on MacDougal Street, as the last six months have been. I may get out to Aunt Beryl's on Long Island for an occasional weekend, but in the main it's going to be almost impossible to get away. My perspective will have to do the best it can."

Dorrie's eyes became more solemn. She could hear the echoes of Jule's and Ella's conversation back in the kitchen and knew from the sudden blotting out of a flickering ball of light on the grass that they had gone to bed. She leaned against the pillar. Her glance rested wistfully on Roger's head, gleaming black in the moonlight, and the profile of his face turned upward to her seemed beautifully young and heroic but very stern. She was a little afraid of that austere mouth.

"I don't know what I'm going to do," she said after a little while. "Linda says there aren't any jobs in Birchfield, and Grandma doesn't want me to go away. Besides I haven't any money."

"You'll write a great deal more poetry, of course," Roger told her firmly. "And you'll send it to me as soon as you've enough for a volume and I'll market it for you. Then, when you've become an established poet, you will come to New York and live, and go to tea with me every Sunday afternoon."

"That would be wonderful," Dorrie acknowledged, but she looked away. Once a week to see her beloved. Oh, no, it would be better almost not to be near him at all than just to be tantalized by his proximity.

"I had no idea these three weeks would be so agreeable," Roger mused, stretching his arms above his head. "I could have gotten things into shape in half the time if I hadn't found this place so pleasant. Of course it's all you. I—I'll miss you frightfully. I don't think you know."

Dorrie spoke with an effort.

"I'll miss you, too, Roger. You see I—I never had anyone to talk to before."

Roger poked the ground with his shoe, absently.

"We'll have to write a lot. I think we need each other's support, really."

"Yes," said Dorrie, her mouth quivering a little. Roger, who had meant to teach her self-sufficiency, had made her forever dependent. Tomorrow he would be miles away, gone, perhaps never to see her again.

"I was thinking—" began Roger, and then stopped short. His lips tightened, for Dorrie, sitting on the step above, had allowed her fingers to droop against his cheek. For an instant he did not move. Then he caught the straying hand and held it tightly to his face. Neither of them spoke, but Dorrie's bosom rose and fell with her quickened breathing. Slowly, Roger raised himself to the place beside her. He took her face in his two hands. Then she was crushed in his arms and his mouth warm upon hers. Breathless, her head drooped back and his kisses fell upon her throat.

"Dorrie—you're—you're so sweet," he whispered. He held her hand gently against his cheek.

"Dorrie—"

"Yes, Roger—" Dorrie's voice was faint. If he would only take her away with him forever—forever!

"Dorrie—honey—"

He drew a long breath, set his jaw grimly, and got to his feet. And then, without another word, he swung abruptly down the steps and across the path to the road. He strode swiftly along, almost as if he were running away from something, and he did not turn around . . .

Dorrie sat just as he had left her, staring down the black road after him. Her throat was throbbing fiercely. She sat very still, a slight white figure in a patch of moonlight. The moon traveled high and lost itself in a forest of black clouds. A wind blew down from the hills and the dew fell. Dorrie was still on the porch steps . . . Dawn came . . . Dorrie slowly stood up. With blurred eyes she fumbled with the latch on the door and went unsteadily into the house.

Chapter Ten

Roger had gone without saying goodbye, but Dorrie told herself he would come back. If New York were a million miles away, he would have to come back . . . But even while she reassured herself, the fear that he had gone forever chilled her heart. She took the walks alone that they had done together, and at each corner or landmark reconstructed what he had said to her and how he had looked. She was careful not to speak of him to Linda or Jule, and no one saw his letter but herself. They were brief formal notes at first; it was a long time before they were even natural.

Sometimes Linda and Jule talked over Dorrie's future. Linda thought she ought to be sent to Columbus to visit Aunt Laura for a while.

"Dorrie's much better than she used to be," she argued, "And it wouldn't hurt Aunt Laura to do something for her. She hasn't written a word since that time she invited me down there."

"You missed your chance there, Linda," observed Ella Morris. "Your aunt would have treated you like a queen. Probably you'd be well-married by this time. No fellows in Birchfield for a girl. None except Courtenay Stall, and my goodness he's too busy running around with fast girls from Cleveland to marry anybody."

"I'm not worried about myself," Linda answered coldly, "I have a good job, anyway. But Dorrie doesn't know a thing except books, and they never get you anywhere. Somebody like Aunt Laura ought to take her in hand. That's the only way she can ever amount to anything."

Jule looked unhappy. She hated to think about big, dark things like futures.

"I guess we'll just let well enough alone," she said comfortably. "Dorrie can stay here and help me, and you never can tell what may come up."

"Looks kinda peaked to me, lately, Dorrie does," Ella ruminated. "Guess that young Lancer hurts her feelings going around with other girls. I remember Dorrie used to think a good deal of him."

"Pooh!" scoffed Linda. "Dorrie doesn't have any feelings."

Linda was thinner and her mouth had a pinched unhappy look. She was twenty-one and already becoming a little bitter. Would nothing ever happen? True, Courtenay spoke to her now, and she and Mary James had resumed a cool, bowing acquaintance. But most of the time Linda was desolate. Nothing mattered, really, anymore. She spoke with her old restraint to Esther Mason, though Esther was no longer an active irritation. She was bad; of course she was bad, but at least she was more discreet about it. She went out of town now for her affairs instead of carrying on under Birchfield's sensitive nose.

Linda leaned on Marie Farley more and more. Marie was quietly happy in her little house on the hill. She only wished her sister and children of New York were here in Birchfield. Fancy trying to raise a family in New York—the worst place in the world. So noisy and dirty. Marie was certainly glad she had had sense enough to get away from it when she did ... Would Aunt Jule look after baby next fall if Marie and Dick could save enough for a fortnight in New York? ...

The only thing that brought Linda any joy was a certain flat packet in the very bottom of her dresser drawer. Sometimes, late at night, Linda had crept out of bed to grope for this trifle, and once having touched it, climbed back into bed, content. No need to reread that letter, for Linda knew every word. It was the letter Courtenay had written her during his brief stay at training camp, before he had been sent home with the bad heart—while he expected to go to France and be heroically killed. When he had come home instead, he had barely looked at Linda. But his note had given her courage.

This was Linda's love letter:

Dear Linda:

Well, I guess you're surprised to hear from me but I wanted to tell you before I went I was sorry about that dance and what happened you know afterward. I didn't mean to start the story but the fellows razzed me so. Hope it didn't make you sore. You sure looked great that night. Well so long.

Yours,
COURTENAY STALL

On their way to an engagement in Marion, Mr. and Mrs. Winslow stopped off at Aunt Jule's. Mrs. Winslow wore the same Gainsborough hat, but she had substituted purple roses for the pink plumes. She kissed Aunt Jule affectionately, patted Dorrie's cheek, and beamed at Linda.

"This will always be home to us," Horace boomed out, leaning on his cane with quite an air. "How many times we've yearned for this delightful spot . . . Ah well, who knows? Someday—"

"Someday we'll have our own dear little place and give up this wearing troupers' life," sighed Mrs. Winslow, her eyes dreamy. "That's all we look forward to, truly, Aunt Jule."

"We're very simple folks," said Horace. "Very simple. A little cottage, a cow, a good collie—"

"If we only could, dear," breathed his wife.

"Of course you can," cried Jule heartily. "Ella was just saying yesterday that the Stalls want to rent their little farm cottage out by Bucyrus for only twelve dollars a month, with a chance to buy it for eight hundred if you like. Dorrie, run up and see if you can get Mr. Stall's office on the phone. He'd be glad to show it to you."

Mr. Winslow put up his hand hastily, and a look of alarm came on his wife's plump, painted face.

"Don't—don't," he begged. "You're too kind. After all, our duty is the stage. *Toujours*. Meaning forever. Our contract, you know. Please, my dear lady, don't make our lot harder by telling us of these tempting opportunities."

"No, please," echoed Mrs. Winslow.

They appeared so uncomfortable that Jule dropped the matter. Dorrie took the little actress aside after a while.

"Mrs. Winslow, I wish you could help me to get on the stage. You see, I don't know how to go about it, but I'm eighteen now and—"

Mrs. Winslow looked at Dorrie with mingled pity and understanding.

"My dear, you're so young. I—I—not that you haven't grown up to be a very pretty young lady since I was here, but the stage is so—well—I—Horace, Dorrie wants us to help her to get on the stage."

Dorrie looked hopefully from one to the other, her hands twisting nervously. Mrs. Winslow glanced at his wife's anxious face and coughed profoundly.

"A worthy ambition—very worthy indeed. Supposing you—er—write us a letter of application, so to speak. I'll see that it—er—reaches the proper person."

His wife looked relieved.

"But I wanted to go right away," Dorrie said, in disappointment. "I know—you don't think I'd be very good at it."

The Winslows hastened to disclaim such a thought. It was only that she was so young and so pretty and had led such a sheltered life that—er—perhaps—their eyes met over Dorrie's wistful face.

"Write the letter, as I suggested, my dear, and you may—there's just a chance, you know—hear from us," urged Mr. Winslow. "And now, my dear wife, we must hurry. Our train is due. Adieu, Miss Shirley, Miss Dorrie, and chère Madame—Adieu!"

* * *

Ella said that of course it wasn't any of her business, and she'd be the last one to make trouble, but was Jule noticing that Mason woman lately? Ella spoke in a low, tense whisper, since you never could tell how strong those kitchen walls were. The couple in the little adjoining suite might be hearing every word.

Jule hesitated a moment before speaking, assuming an expression of benign naivete lest Ella suspect her of knowing more than she pretended.

"A little thinner, perhaps," she said placidly, "but those country girls always lose weight when they come to town to live."

"You know well enough that's not what I mean," Ella rebuked, shaking her finger at the old woman. "You've got eyes in your head. You needn't tell me you haven't seen what she's up to. What I want to know is this—who is the man?"

Jule feigned astonishment. She put down the china egg which had assisted her darning for many decades, and made suitable exclamation.

"She's been going away for days at a time with that straw suitcase of hers," pursued Ella. "She'd like us to believe she's visiting her folks or that cousin of hers in Galion—at least according to her story it's a cousin. But what did her pa say when he brought in those eggs last week? That she hadn't been home once since she'd been married. Acted like she was afraid of the farm, he said. Well!"

"My goodness, Ella!" helplessly protested Jule.

Ella clasped a hand on each arm of her wheelchair and leaned forward impressively.

"She's settled down to one lover, that's what's happened," she declared. "You can't tell me Lew Mason can buy her all those new dresses she's been flaunting lately. That girl's had three hats this season, and I'll bet not one of them cost less than seven dollars. I know this much. She didn't get them at Miss Pearl's shop, so she must have bought them in Galion or maybe Columbus. She's got some rich man she meets every weekend. And if you ask me, I think it's the limit. A disgrace to Birchfield."

Jule cleared her throat. The same idea had been thrust on her recently by Amelia Bellows, and it troubled her. It was so convincing, and everyone seemed to think she ought to do something about it . . . when all she wanted was that everyone, particularly Esther Mason—should be happy and contented. She couldn't dictate to them exactly how they were to be happy, could she?

Ella looked at Jule in steady reproach for a long time. She always warmed up to intimate rebukes and a general family review after eating her beloved tripe. A sense of gentle superiority pervaded her being then, and she was able to give a clearer eye to the faults of her neighbors. Tonight Jule had been moved to make jelly custards, too, so that Ella was never in better form.

Esther Mason, as the raciest item, was the first thing on Ella's list to be settled. After she had disposed of her, she might get around to Linda's bad temper, Dorrie's general shiftlessness, Mrs. Remer's ridiculous pregnancy after fifteen years of respectable sterility, the new Red Cross drive as mismanaged by Mrs. Riggs, and how the mayor himself made her feel a perfect fool holding her hand right in front of his wife the other day. She had planned, loosely, to wind up by being perfectly frank with Jule as one old friend to another about the way the house was cared for, and what changes she would like to recommend.

But for the moment Esther Mason's affairs held the floor.

"She's such a sweet little thing," Jule defended. "I can't see a bit of harm in her. Maybe a little high-spirited, but then she's young."

"Well there is harm in her," retorted Ella, unsympathetically.

"I've been hearing lots of things about that young woman lately. What's more, everybody says it's your fault. You ought to be a mother to her and tell her what's what when she doesn't do right by her husband . . . A lover! . . . At her age! . . . Why, she isn't even twenty years old!"

"But she's seen a lot of life," Jule said, unwisely. Ella clicked expressively.

"I should say she has! Running around with all the boys in town . . . And now this man, whoever he is, buying her hats and dresses!"

Jule wiped her spectacles on her apron and made a great business of polishing them.

"I'm sure," she began feebly, "I'm sure people don't understand Esther. She's just a lighthearted little thing, and she doesn't see any harm in what she's doing. A little weak, maybe."

"Weak?" grunted Ella. "Weak? That girl's strong, let me tell you. It's the men who are weak. Why, there isn't a man in town with character enough to stand still when she smirks at 'em. They run after her like dumb sheep. That's the man of it."

The back door opened and Linda came in listlessly. She'd been taking care of Marie's baby while Marie and Dick went to the movies. It always made her unhappy to sit in their little living room alone with their baby and know that these solid, respectable things were so far, far away from her own life. It did not cheer her any to find Ella and Jule engaged in their eternal gossip there in the kitchen.

"You two!" she exclaimed, sarcastically. "I suppose you've been talking me over while I was out. What's the latest gossip of Linda Shirley, Ella? I'm sure you must know."

"We didn't even mention your name," Ella replied tartly, her eyes sparkling with indignation. "If you want to know, we were simply referring to what people say about Esther Mason."

Linda sat down in a chair by the dining room table and leaned her face wearily on her elbow.

"What is it now?" she demanded. "Ran off and left Lew, I suppose. I wish to goodness she would."

"No," Ella explained, ignoring Jule's furtive signals. "She's likely to find herself put out though, if she isn't careful. She's been going off for days at a stretch with some well-to-do fellow who buys her clothes and such."

"What!"

To Linda the fact that Esther should receive reward for her misdemeanors was more horrible than the sin itself.

"Just what I was telling Aunt Jule," Ella went on. "If somebody doesn't say something to the girl, Lew's going to put her out. Husbands don't mind their wives running around with a lot of men, but when it gets down to just one lover, they get insulted. Yes, sir. Lew Mason'll probably stone her out of town if he finds out. A man always likes to make an example of his wife."

"Who is the man?" Linda asked, with vague curiosity.

"I don't know," Ella registered profoundest regret. "It's somebody with enough money for a car and old enough to know where to take her. But Mrs. Miller was saying just the other day—somehow the talk got around to this place and how I happened to stay on here, considering the talk there's always been—and she was saying she was sure it was none of our Birchfield boys. She thought it might be one of the railroad men that stop at Red's shack for lunch. They're a pretty fast lot. On the other hand it might be one of the young men around town. I've heard a lot of talk about it. Esther's such a forward girl—prancing up and down the streets every night so that nobody could help talking about her."

"Well, Grandmother, don't you think it's time you told the Masons to clear out?" Linda asked indignantly. "Haven't we put up with this sort of thing long enough?"

"Hush—hush—" Jule soothed, a little worried frown appearing on her broad brow. "I'll see that she behaves herself. I'll speak to her."

She polished her spectacles with even more absorption, well aware of the contemptuous doubt in Linda's and Ella's eyes. Ella vibrated suddenly with a new and thrilling idea. Her eyes glowed, and she sent a sly, speculative glance in Linda's direction.

"Why not have Linda talk to her?" she suggested brightly. "I'm sure she'd pay more attention to what Linda said than anything you could say, Jule Shirley. You're too soft to handle a woman like that."

"No, I'll speak to Esther," Jule promised hastily. "Tomorrow."

"Well, if you don't, I will," Linda threatened.

And when, a week later, Marie Farley asked Linda if it were true that Mayor Riggs was Esther Mason's lover, she did speak to Esther.

* * *

Linda told herself she must be very calm when she called on Esther. That was always the best way—to be very calm and aloof. Then the girl wouldn't dare to argue with her. She would go in on a Saturday, she thought, when Lew was out, and say very briefly that the house was being talked about as the result of Esther's behavior and therefore her grandmother wanted Esther to leave at once.

Esther was in a pink crepe kimono, lolling on the bed which almost filled the dingy little bedroom. She had a bag of cheap candies at her side and was reading one of the old *People's Home Journals* that Jule had cleared out of the pantry cupboard. The lace curtain at the little window next to the shed was caught back to admit a few more rays of reluctant sunshine into the room. Esther was often caught yanking furiously at the curtain in her zeal for sunshine, and today Linda noted mechanically that the lace was hanging in shreds.

She listened with mouth agape to Linda's stiff little speech. She was so genuinely astonished that it did not occur to her to argue the matter of her virtue or her person as a subject for scandal. She accepted the sentence and considered it, lying back on the pillows, her bold black eyes fixed on Linda.

"But how can I go?" she asked presently. "What can I tell Lew?"

"I don't care what you tell Lew," Linda replied. "I'm sure you've told him enough lies when you've gone off before and left him."

"Yes, but I always came back before," Esther said virtuously. "Say, what are you so anxious to get me out of the way for? I never hurt you any. What's the idea?"

"You've hurt me enough," Linda muttered savagely. She stood straight and unyielding in the doorway, a slim rod of steel. "You are going, then?"

"Yes, I may go," Esther said, a secret smile playing about her full red lips. "My friend can take care of me, I guess."

Linda's chiseled face showed her disgust at the allusion. Esther dropped languidly back on the pillows, one leg swinging off at the side of the bed. She eyed Linda with a subtle insolence.

"Maybe you'd like to know who he is," she invited. "I've heard you and that old harpy in there wondering about my business. 'Who is he?'" she mimicked Linda's voice and then Ella's shrill soprano, "'Some rich fellow that buys her clothes.' Bah! Why don't you get a thrill of your own instead of living on mine?"

"I've never been interested in your affairs," Linda stated, raging inwardly. She wanted to go right now, but some curious impulse made her linger.

Esther gazed coyly at the ceiling.

"I should think you would be interested," she said. "It don't take half an eye to see that you're crazy about the man yourself." Linda turned slowly to the other girl. A strange misgiving trickled through her nerves. It caused her to brace herself involuntarily against the door.

"Maybe you do know," purred Esther spitefully. "Maybe that's why you're ordering me out of the house. You know he's crazy about me and it makes you sore."

Linda tried to speak but her throat clicked inarticulately. Her hand grasped the doorknob. The blood left her face. Oh, no, that—*that* could not be. Her hero . . . Her god . . . No, no, no!

"He's wonderful," Esther sighed tantalizingly, hooking her hands over her raised knee. "And oh, how he can make love! But I don't suppose he ever even kissed you."

"I don't know what you're talking about," Linda said huskily, maddened by that knowledge in the other's black eyes.

"Oh yes, you do," Esther mocked. "You know what I mean. You're crazy, crazy about Courtenay Stall, but he's my lover. Understand? He's my lover."

"Oh, you—!" The cry was torn from Linda's heart. That she should have to face this woman! That she should have to hear her boast—yes, boast of Courtenay Stall as her lover! And oh, that she should be shamed in her soul by envy—envy that swept her from head to foot—black, overwhelming envy of a prostitute!

"Get out of this house!" she shrieked, stamping her foot on the floor. "Never dare to say such things to me again! He doesn't love you, he only takes you because you're cheap and common . . ."

Esther's eyes flashed.

"Oh, he can take who he pleases," she drawled, "as you know. But he loves me, you see. *Me*. And if I do as you say and divorce Lew—"

"I didn't tell you to divorce Lew," Linda cried.

Esther smiled.

"—I'll marry Courtenay Stall . . . If I care to," Esther studied her fingernails. "Perhaps I won't care to. Maybe I'll just tell him where to get off. It's been almost as tiresome as being married, going out with just one man all these months. He won't let me have any other friends. Jealous."

She stretched herself impudently and yawned in Linda's outraged face. Linda stood rigidly against the door, her hand clutching the knob, breathing sharply.

"Go away—get out!" she commanded, but her voice was only a hoarse whisper, and she could not bring herself to look at the other girl.

Esther wriggled lazily to her feet, a mocking smile still on her lips. She hummed a fragment of "Caroline" and cocked her head tantalizingly at Linda.

"Oh, I'll go, don't worry," she drawled. "I'd rather go someplace else anyway and have my fun than stay here and be bothered by you and that nasty old cripple."

"You're not to see Courtenay Stall again, do you hear?" Linda's voice was edged with sharp fury. "You're bad—bad—bad, and if you don't leave him alone I'll—I'll—"

"What'll you do?" taunted Esther.

"I'll kill you," Linda breathed.

Esther's mouth dropped open, and her dark eyes grew large in astonishment.

"My—my, you are jealous, aren't you?" she said, softly. "Wouldn't think you cared that much for anyone but yourself. I'll have to tell—"

Before she could finish the sentence, Linda took a menacing step forward, her fists clenched at her side, her blue eyes sparkling fire. Esther stopped short, instinctively put up an arm before her face, and backed against the wall.

"Don't you dare speak that name again! Never! Get—out—of—this—house! If you don't—"

Her body relaxed, and she drew a long breath. Esther calmly took out a bureau drawer and dumped its contents on the bed. She dragged a dusty suitcase from the closet . . . Linda backed slowly to the door, turned the knob and went out. As the door closed behind her, Esther's voice rose in shrill defiance.

"You wish he was your lover, Linda Shirley! You wish he was yours!"

But Linda, white and shaken, stumbled on to her room.

* * *

Jule never quite understood how Esther Mason could disappear so suddenly. Lew came to her in sodden despair and begged her to help him find his wayward darling. All she needed was a good beating and she'd be as good as gold. She was bad but then he was bad, too. He didn't mind saying so. Lew mopped his eyes freely with a red handkerchief, and his face was bloated with tears.

"Her folks say she ain't out there," he moaned. "They blamed me for not holding her in tighter. I figured, you see, I'd let her have her head the first lap and let her get winded, then she'd have to settle down to a sensible jog-trot."

Jule was helpless. Her own spectacles were clouded with her tears, and she tried vaguely consoling remarks. Esther had completely vanished. Red Turner had seen her get on a westbound train, but the station agent said she hadn't bought a ticket. Where she had gone no one could guess, or even the reason for her going.

That Linda might have had something to do with the affair did occur to Jule later on in the day, after Dorrie had remarked on Linda's absence at supper. Then Jule recalled that Linda had been in her room with the door locked since noon.

"Hm," she said, her brows puckering. She was tremendously relieved that Ella was dining out with the Remers that night. It postponed talk till tomorrow at least.

"Maybe she'll be back tonight," she told Lew, who sat, a great lump of despair on the shoebox in the kitchen corner, his watery eyes fastened with dogged hope on Jule. "What if she did take all her clothes and leave a note? Women have changed their minds before this."

Lew shook his head.

"Yes, but she won't. She don't do things that way. Nope. If that gal's gone, she's gone." Saying it seemed to relieve him, and he got laboriously to his feet and swayed on them for an instant. "Might as well make up my mind to it. I'll stick to my horses and let women go to blazes. A horse knows a good master but a woman don't."

He was visibly cheered at the thought of his horses, and the whisky he had taken for moral support now began to take effect. His chest swelled and he thumped it.

"Yes, sir. Give me a horse, every time. Why, Aunt Jule, you couldn't pay me to take that woman back. I wouldn't have the dirty hussy."

He marched to the door, and the back of his neck was livid with the slow rage that was coming over him. "I wouldn't have her if you gave me ten horses . . . no, not for twenty horses!"

The door banged behind him, but in a moment it opened to reveal his sorrowful, bloated face.

"Aunt Jule," he whimpered. "If—if she comes back, you tell her I'm living over in the loft again . . . I'll be there."

"Poor old Lew," Jule murmured. "He was lucky to have her while he did. A pretty little thing like that."

Dorrie wasn't sorry for Lew. Nor could she feel sorry for the lost Esther. Esther had probably set off gloriously, deliriously for perdition and was doubtless far happier in her untrammeled sinning than Birchfield was in its virtues.

* * *

That night Mrs. Will Stall came to Aunt Jule's. Her mission was neither to see Amelia Bellows or Esther Morris. She stood, embarrassed and nervous, outside the screen door and asked in a low voice if she might see Mrs. Lew Mason. A large, impressive figure was Mrs. Stall, and a white-haired middle age had given a dignity to her features that they of themselves did not possess. The front of Jule's house was unlighted, but the lamps from the Stall automobile in the lane silhouetted the caller's unmistakable lines.

Linda had tiptoed downstairs while the others were in the kitchen to sit in the dark cool living room. It was she who answered the light knock on the door. At sight of Mrs. Stall, cloaked, with a dark scarf flung over her hair, Linda stared unbelievingly. She could see beyond her the lights of the Stall car with Gertrude's motionless figure at the wheel.

Mutely, she opened the door. It did not occur to her to turn on the gaslights, so the two women stood there inside the doorway, dimly illumined by the auto lamp, their faces almost invisible to each other.

"Mrs. Mason is not here," Linda said, a vibrant triumph in her voice. "She has left town."

The older woman sat down heavily in a chair. The scarf fell back from her head and she mechanically put up a hand to adjust a strand of hair.

"Left town?" she repeated stupidly. "Do you mean she has gone away with Courtenay?"

"No!" Linda cried, aghast. "Oh, Mrs. Stall, how could you think of such a thing?"

Mrs. Stall made a gesture of weariness.

"Don't be sarcastic, please. I want to know if they've gone off together, if she really has gone. I didn't know that. I thought I might talk to her tonight. But you say she's left. Court's not home, either . . . I should have come last week or even sooner. Only it's hard to know what to do . . . Court's so heady. If I'd interfered before, likely enough he would have run off with the woman." She laughed shortly. "And now he's done it, anyway."

"No, he didn't go with her," Linda said eagerly. "He drove past with the Lancer boys this morning to the football game in Marion. And she—I sent her away this afternoon on the train."

"You sent her?" Mrs. Stall's pale gray eyes narrowed. She leaned forward and peered up at Linda's dim face. "Why did you do that?"

Linda forgot it was Mrs. Will Stall she was addressing. Supported by the hate she felt toward Esther Mason, she could have spoken to queens without hesitation.

"She's bad, Mrs. Stall," she said passionately. "Courtenay couldn't help himself, because she's such a bad woman."

"I'm afraid he could have," Mrs. Stall answered, skeptically. "I've had so much trouble with that boy. Spoiled . . . And now this awful woman . . . the talk of the town . . . I had to do something. You never can do a thing with Court so . . . so I came to her . . . Will said not to, but I thought if I gave her a little money to go away . . . Court's as bad as she is, only—"

"Oh, how can you say so?" Linda flared in hushed indignation. "He is so fine, such a fine, true man—"

"I'm afraid Court has a great many weaknesses," Mrs. Stall broke in.

Linda, in the darkness, bent down to Mrs. Stall, her young face drawn with emotion.

"Courtenay's not weak, Mrs. Stall," she said vehemently. "It's all that woman. She's black as sin, and no man could help himself when she got him in her clutches. No, no—you shan't say anything about Courtenay Stall."

The older woman sat very still.

"I'm his mother, you know," she said, in a queer strained voice. "It's natural that I should know his faults."

"Oh, you don't understand him," Linda cried hysterically. "Can't you see how fine he is—fine all the way through? He wouldn't do these things of his own accord. He's—he's—"

And then she collapsed feebly, a crumpled heap of gray against the black of the walls.

Mrs. Stall groped through the darkness to her side and raised her head. Linda's face was a dim white blot in the dark room.

"You're all worn out, my dear," Mrs. Stall's voice was puzzled but kind. "I think you need a rest. I'm glad you sent the girl away. Perhaps my son did not go with her, after all. Perhaps—perhaps he is as good as you believe he is."

Linda gave a faint moan. She tried weakly to rise.

"I'll call someone from the back of the house to come in to you," the woman said, quickly. "You're not well. I'll rap on the back door and then dip out to my car—"

"No, please," Linda took command of herself at once. No one in Jule's house must know of this interview. It was hers. She stood up, clinging a little to the other woman's arm.

"You're sure—"

"I'm perfectly all right," Linda whispered. "I'll go upstairs and go to bed."

She felt Mrs. Stall's hand touching hers in a slight clasp.

"Good night, Linda. And—thank you."

The older woman opened the door and hurried down to the waiting motor, but she turned at the gate to look backward, her face thoughtful and wondering.

* * *

All day Sunday Linda stayed in bed. Dorrie brought up coffee and toast to her room and looked at her curiously. It may not have occurred to Jule that Linda had sent Esther Mason away, but Dorrie had her own suspicions. Seeing Linda limp, with eyes shadowed with purple from a night of tears, was sufficient evidence for Dorrie.

"Tell Grandmother I have a bad headache," Linda asked of Dorrie, turning her face quickly to the wall. "I won't be down."

Dorrie went away, and Linda buried her face in the pillow and lay still for a long time. She had boldly defended Courtenay to his own mother—as if she had the right. Actually defying the woman—telling her that she didn't know her own son! . . . Linda blushed, aghast at the memory of her own daring. How could she have done such a thing? . . . But Mrs. Stall had been kind . . . There was a bond between them now—a bond where there had been a wall.

"She will always be friends with me," Linda thought, "because I saved her son. But he—he—"

He, Courtenay, would never look at her again. That was the thing that left Linda wretched and hopeless. She had sent away Esther Mason because that person dared to have Courtenay Stall for a lover. But what would the lover say to Linda Shirley's interference? If there had been hope of his friendship before, certainly yesterday's events would shut her out from his world forever.

"Oh, it isn't my fault, it isn't—it isn't," Linda moaned into her pillow, her body rigid with pent-up anguish. "I had to send her away . . . Mrs. Stall thought I did right . . . *She* understood . . . But she will tell Courtenay it was I who interfered in the affair, and he will hate me. He will never look at me. Or perhaps he will go after Esther . . . If he is the way his mother says he is—heady—perhaps I did just the thing to make him fall deeper in love with her."

A shudder ran through her. After a while she lay on her side and looked out the window over the birches. Sun filtered through the curtains and palpitated on the carpet.

"Nothing has been my fault," Linda thought drearily. "If we had only lived in a proper neighborhood and with respectable people, this would never have happened. Perhaps—perhaps Courtenay might have fallen in love with me long ago. It's Grandmother's fault for keeping this place and bringing us up in the midst of such awful people, so that everyone had to shun us. It's her fault."

But that did not make the present hour any easier. Linda jumped out of bed impatiently and jerked down the window shades. The sunlight on the birches irritated her eyes. She wanted darkness since her own life had suddenly become so dark.

"I've ruined everything now," she told herself bitterly. "When his mother tells him about me he will want to kill me."

What if Mrs. Will Stall had discovered that there was one person in the black house beyond the tracks who stood for the same respectability that Birchfield itself represented? What was that to Linda, if in order to gain respectability she was to lose her life dream?

"I've wrecked my whole life," she muttered. "Nothing, nothing can ever come to me now."

She crawled back into bed and lay there motionless on her face for hours. She heard Dorrie calling her to come down to dinner, but she pretended to be asleep and made no answer . . . And then, mercifully enough, she did go to sleep.

It was late afternoon when she woke up. She rubbed her eyes, bewildered, trying to remember the awful thing that had made waking so futile for her . . . Esther . . . Mrs. Stall . . . Courtenay . . .

"Linda," she heard Dorrie's voice raised outside her door. "What is the matter? Can't you hear me?"

Linda raised herself on one elbow.

"Well?" she asked resignedly.

"I've knocked three times," Dorrie told her. "Open the door. There's someone downstairs to see you."

The thought of Mary James's pale crafty face flitted through Linda's mind. Even seeing Marie Farley would be galling to her now.

"I don't feel well enough to see anyone," she whimpered. "I'm not going to come down. Tell her to go away. I'll—I'll telephone her when I feel better."

"It isn't Marie," Dorrie retorted in a stage whisper. "It's Courtenay Stall. He's in the hall and he wants to see you."

Linda reeled out of bed, clasping her head. He couldn't really be downstairs. Dorrie was making it up. Or perhaps she herself was dreaming.

"Did you—did you say—" she began.

"I did," Dorrie interrupted with suppressed excitement. "So you'd better hurry."

Hurry? Linda's hands were clammy with nervousness, and her legs were slow and heavy, as if they belonged to someone else and she had no power over them. She knocked over the trays and jars on her dressing table in her frantic attempt at haste. She twisted her hair about her head and saw helplessly that it was loose and there were disorderly wisps flying about her pallid skin . . . She sat down on the bed, holding her head tightly, trying to remember which dress was her best one . . . Of course, the green crepe de chine. She slipped it over her head with trembling hands and then ran to the staircase, stumbling a little and feeling uncertain and weak as to her legs.

Courtenay was standing in the hall, his eyes on the floor. He looked nervous and uncomfortable, twisting his hat in his hands and occasionally stroking his reddish hair with quick, restless movements. Today there was something quiet and chastened in his bearing that was not at all like the young Stall the village blades knew.

"Linda, I thought—" he began awkwardly, "I thought you might— well, if you haven't anything to do, we might go for a ride in the old car."

Linda's body seemed to gain instant strength. Her blood warmed. She tingled and throbbed with the dizzy realization that he had come to her. He had come to her at last.

"I'll get my coat," she said and ran back up the stairs.

She was scarcely conscious of Ella's curious eyes peering at her through the curtains as she and Courtenay walked out toward the road. She knew that Dorrie and Jule were surely whispering back there in the living room, wondering how this strange event had come to pass. But it was far in the back of her brain. All she was absolutely sure of was that she was walking close to Courtenay Stall's side across the road, and now being helped by his large, strong hands into the seat of his roadster.

Courtenay swung over the door into the place at the wheel. She warmed at the intimacy of his silence. They glided down the road to the main highway, Courtenay absorbed in the business of driving, and Linda in a haze of happiness.

It was a long time before he spoke.

"Have a lot to thank you for, Linda, I guess . . . I kinda lose my head sometimes. Do things I could kick myself for afterward. You know. Like that night at the dance . . . And then—well, the Mason woman. I was—well, may as well out with it—I suppose—I was in pretty deep there. She's—"

He paused and Linda softly put in, "She's bad, I understand."

Courtenay looked a little relieved. He kept his eyes on the road ahead.

"Well, she's not good enough to be in the same house with you anyway," he said in an embarrassed undertone. "But you wouldn't need to have gotten mixed up with her if—if you hadn't wanted to protect me. I know all right. Ma told me you sent her off and how you stuck up for me . . . I almost dropped dead . . . You know . . . Struck me kinda funny that a girl should be sticking up for me to my own mother. Kinda—well—white. Made me feel like a fool . . . Ashamed as the deuce . . . have a girl like you bothering her head over me. Rotten business . . . I told Ma I was going to tell you a thing or two. Ha, ha! She thought I was mad."

Linda looked at him, her blue eyes brimming with a wondering joy. She could not speak. They whirred past farmhouses and hilly fields, russet under the setting sun. She felt her hair blowing about her face but the untidiness of it did not disturb her. She was happy. She was swayed toward him at a sharp turn in the road.

"You're—you're a mighty fine girl, Linda," Courtenay said unevenly, his face flushing a little. He slipped an arm over her shoulders and Linda allowed it to stay. "I—I've thought a lot more about you since that party than you know. Only—oh, well, I'm no good, you know. Always was useless. Always will be."

"No," Linda whispered. "You're splendid." Courtenay grinned sheepishly.

"Maybe I would be if you'd look after me. I mean—" he coughed and grew very red, "you know—ha, ha!—be Mrs. Stall Junior."

Linda's lips parted and she looked dewily at him.

"When, Courtenay?" she asked. Courtenay kissed her hotly. Later on, Linda thought, after they were married, she could tell him she didn't like to be kissed.

Chapter Eleven

Dorrie leaned on the attic windowsill and watched the apple blossoms fluttering down from the tree. Sometimes she stretched out a hand absently to catch some of the pale petals and press their softness against her cheek. She could see the trains dash by, leaving a fog of gray smoke to settle slowly over the birch trees. Sometimes the trains stopped, panting impatience, and left strangers on the platform . . . These Dorrie studied eagerly because one of them might be . . . might be . . . it never was, but someday it would be Roger. He would stride swiftly up from the station and she would whirl down the road to meet him . . .

In the backyard Jule, a shawl thrown over her head, poked encouragement at sullen vegetables in the weedy garden patch. Dorrie could hear her mellow voice exchanging comments with Ella sitting in the kitchen, and she could hear Ella's shrill monologue, the monologue that had been going on ever since Linda's wedding day had been set.

"You can't get a word out of Linda," Ella was saying heatedly. "She always was closemouthed, but since she got engaged to Courtenay Stall last fall you can't get a word—not one word. I said to her this morning, I said, Linda, how does it feel to have a wedding day coming on? Another week and you'll be Mrs. Stall, I said. She just looked at me. Ella, she said, if you'd just as soon I'd rather not talk about it. It isn't the sort of thing, she said, it isn't the sort of thing I want all over town. You'd think I hadn't the slightest particle of friendly interest in her, the way she acted. As if I hadn't known the Stalls a sight longer than she has."

"Of course," Jule's voice soothed. "It seems to me I planted some seeds here but nothing's coming up. I thought we might have some sweet corn this year—just a few stalks, you know."

"It'd be up now if it's going to come up at all," Ella replied shortly and then, "But let me tell you, Jule Shirley, Linda needn't think she's going to come between me and my friends. It's her doing that I never heard from Mrs. Stall about the engagement till the wedding day was almost here . . . I don't understand that girl. Never did. I shouldn't be surprised if she was jealous about me too. I notice Courtenay hasn't dropped in for a talk for weeks. Just walks right out with Linda. You'd think I hadn't known him since he was in short pants . . . My goodness, there's never been a thing between Courtenay and me, really. Not a thing. Of course he used to drop in all hours of the night and talk but as for—well, getting personal, no— not a bit. Courtenay's as much a gentleman as his father. No matter how fast they may be—and there's no getting around that fact, one's as bad as the other—they both know a lady when they see one and know how to treat her . . . I've never had a bit of trouble with either Will or Courtenay."

Jule stooped over and selected one unfortunate weed among the thousands for uprooting. Her back creaked and she stood for a minute resting. She put a hand up over her eyes and looked up toward the attic window.

"Dorrie," she called, "are you up there? Have you put the hem in that dress from Laura? Get Judy to help you with the hanging."

"I will," promised Dorrie, but she did not stir for a long time.

When Roger came back this summer he would see her in the taffeta dress Aunt Laura had sent her. He would say, "Dorrie, how beautiful you have become!" He would take her away to New York and eastern cities, and she would be smooth and silky like Claire Moffatt. She didn't mind waiting for him—it prolonged the delight of thinking about it

. . . And if he didn't come this summer, then surely he would come this fall. Things happened that way . . . Aunt Laura would send her a pink velvet dress to wear. Aunt Laura had written, on being apprised of Linda's wedding, that it was just as she had said. Linda was marrying one of those bumpkins and nobody could say she hadn't warned Mother that she'd do just that very thing. A girl like Linda marrying Birchfield when if Jule had only had the sense to send her to Columbus when she, Laura, had wanted her, she could have had her pick of senators and millionaires. But the thing was done. All she could do now was to send her congratulations and a box of clothes, including a simple white satin wedding dress for Linda and a perfectly new taffeta for Dorrie. Aunt Laura added that she did hope Jule would try and use a little more discretion about Dorrie. There was no excuse for a girl of any intelligence marrying stupid men anymore when if she used her head, she could take her choice of really worthwhile men.

Linda hadn't minded the insinuations or the truly insulting tenor of Aunt Laura's letter since the gowns she had sent were so beautiful, an index of Aunt Laura's increasing prosperity rather than her good wishes. There was even a leghorn hat for Dorrie to wear at the garden party—a floppy affair with ribbons of orchid taffeta to match her gown. And there were all manner of dainty underthings for Linda. Jule had puttered over Linda's stockings and made several good stout petticoats that refused to look festive even when coaxed with a lace and baby-ribbon edging. She was not surprised that Linda should marry into one of Birchfield's leading families. Why not? Linda was as pretty a girl as the town had ever boasted of. Why shouldn't she win whomsoever she had decided upon? Nor was she offended that the Stalls should ignore the amenities and take complete charge of her granddaughter's wedding without consulting her in any detail.

Mrs. Will Stall was taking care that Birchfield should be pacified by explaining that her daughter-in-law's connections *outside* Birchfield were of the highest—Theodore Shirley, you know, probably Ohio's next senator, and Mrs. Richard Tooley of Columbus. Oh yes, Mrs. Stall made it plain that her son's marriage was not at all the subject for scandal which the village was at first tempted to believe. Since the thing was settled and there was nothing to be done about it, she was doing her best to make it appear the most desirable match in the world. And after all, she soon recognized in Linda a soul akin to her own . . .

Dorrie went slowly down to the kitchen. Jule had come in from the garden for a cup of coffee and Ella was seizing the opportunity to criticize the two lady acrobats occupying the little suite Esther Mason once had.

"They're bad, those actresses," Ella whispered, warningly. "If Linda ever finds out you let those girls come here again, there'll be some fine music, let me tell you. Listen to them."

"Now, now, Ella, don't be hasty," Jule remonstrated. "A couple of mighty plucky little girls! Taking hold the way they have with everything against them. I call it mighty plucky—mighty plucky indeed. Their show broken up and no money to get back to New York or anything. I call it mighty plucky of them to keep their nerve."

"Yes, you would say that," Ella retorted. "It's a good thing Linda's not paying attention to what goes on here anymore!"

"They're good hardworking girls, Judy and Birdie are," Jule said. "They've been stopping here for years."

Ella sniffed.

"That doesn't say so much for their character. Listen to them swearing and talking the way they do." There was a sound of laughter from the other side of the kitchen partition. Ella frowned. "Who's that? Do you hear that man's voice in there with those girls?"

"Oh, that's just Miss Bellow's brother," Jule explained blandly. "He's here for a few days and I suppose Judy invited him in to have a bite with them. Gets kinda lonesome for them."

"So that's the new man in the north room." Ella looked at Julie in steady reproach. "Why didn't you say so in the first place? Came yesterday didn't he? My goodness, Jule, you're getting closemouthed! As bad as Linda. What's he doing here? I thought he was in business in Akron with that automobile concern."

"It didn't do so well," Jule said, a guilty flush creeping over her brown withered cheeks. "It seems they had a very bad year."

"Of course," scornfully echoed Ella, "of course they had a bad year. I knew they would. I suppose he's back on his sister's hands again. Raising Cain with those actresses, too, as soon as he found out their first names."

Dorrie opened the door of the adjoining kitchenette, the taffeta dress she was to wear to Linda's wedding over her arm.

"Tell Judy," Jule called after her, "to help you make a nice red rose for the waist. It'll brighten up the dress . . . Laura never had a bit of style."

As the door closed on her granddaughter, a peal of shrill laughter and a rich curse in Birdie's husky baritone made the thin partition vibrate. Jule hurriedly threw her shawl over her head and picked up the garden basket again.

"Oh!" gasped Ella, her eyes popping. "Did you hear that, Jule Shirley? Did you hear what that girl said?"

Jule was out the back door.

"I'm going to look at that corn again," she murmured. "I think we'll have a real garden this year."

About the Author

Dawn Powell (1896–1965) was the prolific writer of sixteen novels, scores of short stories, plays, and more. She was born in Mount Gilead, Ohio, and moved into her aunt's boardinghouse after running away from her father and abusive stepmother. She left Ohio after graduating college and moved to Manhattan, but she returned to the region of her upbringing in much of her writing. She is known for her social satire that is unflinching and humorous without being malicious. Ernest Hemingway called her his "favorite living writer."

Belt Publishing
beltpublishing.com